D0594382

THE DARE SISTERS:
SHIPWRECKED

THE DARE SISTERS: SHIPWRECKED

Jess Rinker

[Imprint]
MAKE YOUR MARK
New York

[Imprint]
MAKE YOUR MARK

A part of Macmillan Children's Publishing Group, LLC
120 Broadway, New York, NY 10271

Library of Congress Control Number: 2021906529

ISBN 978-1-250-21340-2 (hardcover) / ISBN 978-1-250-21341-9 (ebook)

Our books may be purchased in bulk for promotional, educational, or business use. Please contact your local bookseller or the Macmillan Corporate and Premium Sales Department at (800) 221-7945 ext. 5442 or by e-mail at MacmillanSpecialMarkets@macmillan.com.

Book design by Carolyn Bull

Imprint logo designed by Amanda Spielman

First edition, 2022

1 3 5 7 9 10 8 6 4 2

mackids.com

'Tis true this little book contains
Countless secrets and treasures untold:
Codes and keys, riddles and games
About shiny pirates gold.
So, should you fail to heed due dates,
Or pilfer, and ruin sales—Avast,
Scallywag! Lest ye suffer dark fates!
For dead men tell no tales.

For Becca, and all sisters who adventure together

THE DARE SISTERS:
SHIPWRECKED

The Graveyard of the Atlantic

October 1996

"A strong, salty breeze rippled through the sails of the *Adventure*. Some of Blackbeard's crew thought it was a bad omen, as the sea was otherwise calm." I pretend to read from an old, worn leather journal that belonged to my grandfather, Cornelius Franklin Dare, the famous treasure hunter. Well, famous, at least, to my family.

We're all gathered on and around a sandy picnic table under a big live oak near the campground. Several families are still visiting our village on Ocracoke Island, North Carolina, even though the vacation season is just about over, and we decided to practice some ghost stories on the kids. Everyone's eyes focus on me, "Savvy" Savannah Mae, as I talk. "The pirates had always been fortunate, but now some feared the worst. Evil was lurking."

My older sister, Frankie, who at thirteen, still thinks

she's the boss of me, pulls the book down from my face. "Savannah," she says, "it's getting late. Could you get to the point?"

"Shhh!" I lift the book back up and keep pretending to read. "Despite the omen, everyone on board was more interested in having a party. They didn't really think anything bad could ever happen to them. Edward Teach, least of all. He was the captain of the *Adventure* and the most feared pirate of all. In fact, he was the captain of some of the most famous pirates in the Graveyard of the Atlantic and beyond! He was Blackbeard, himself."

One of the boys, with a very dirty face, raises his hand. "Why is there a graveyard in the Atlantic?"

My little sister, Jolene, stands up and wiggles her fingers. "It's because there are so many sailor ghosts haunting the sea, me hearties!" She tries to sound scary, but she's only six and too cute to be very scary. Even with the pirate eye patch she's wearing, she still looks like a tiny angel with corn silk hair.

Several grown-ups—all tourists—ride by on bikes, waving as they pass. The sand crunches under their tires. One lady says, "Alex, one hour, and then we're heading over to the lighthouse before sunset."

The boy with the dirty face, Alex, ducks his head a little bit. "Okay, Mom."

Frankie stands up and starts to dust the sand off herself and Jolene. "The truth is, all along the coast of

North Carolina there have been thousands of shipwrecks. So it's called the Graveyard," Frankie explains.

"It's because the water is so shallow," my cousin Peter adds. He leans against a walking stick our grandpa carved a long time ago. "Lots of ships hit bottom or got caught in storms over the centuries." The other kids nod with interest. We've totally got them hook, line, and sinker. As long as Frankie doesn't stop me while I'm on a roll. She has a habit of interrupting.

Right on cue, my best friend, Kate, asks, "Savvy? What does your grandfather's journal say about Blackbeard's death?" She sounds a little fake, but I don't think anyone else notices her bad acting.

I scan the page, pretending to search it for answers. In reality, the book is only Grandpa's sailing log from 1960 to 1965. It looks old and official, but it doesn't actually say anything about Blackbeard, or pirates at all. Like my pirate costume, I'm using the book as a prop for effect. But the story I'm telling is mostly true, so it's not lying. Not exactly. *Embellishing,* Mom would say. Adding details to a true story to make it more exciting. She says that Grandpa did it all the time but that I probably should be careful when I embellish, especially in my homework.

The page in Grandpa's book actually says: "Cape Lookout Port. Docked 11:34am." But I point to it and say, "*Oh!* It says here . . . Blackbeard was murdered!"

All the kids around me gasp, including Kate, who said she'd help freak out everyone else, and she's great at the gasping part. Only Frankie and Jolene and Peter are quiet, because they already know this whole story. I look up into the eyes of nine other kids I never knew before today, all enraptured with the best version of Blackbeard's story I could create.

I charged them only a dollar apiece. We're waiting for our home—which Grandpa named the Queen Mary after our grandma, as if it were a ship—to be approved in the historical registry. This will make our house a historical site that no one can take from us, like the scallywag Dunmore Throop tried last month. Dad said every little bit could help, so I intend to do my part and donate our profit to the bills. Eventually, I plan to start my own ghost story business for kids, complete with tours around our small village.

I turn the page. "Yes, it says here he was pardoned by the government for his crime of robbery, but Robert Maynard killed him anyway. So it was murder."

"How did he do it?" Kate whispers, hitting her next cue perfectly.

"Well"—I lower my voice and walk around the circle of kids—"first they had an epic sword fight on the deck of the *Adventure*. And then Blackbeard was shot twenty times and unable to defend himself any longer. Maynard cut off his head and threw his body into the ocean." Then I whisper and lean in like I'm telling them the biggest secret they will ever hear in their entire lives. "Then Blackbeard's body circled the boat nine times before it finally sank. It was never found again. And"—I pause for extra effect—"it might still be out there."

One little boy shivers.

Frankie mumbles, "That's a great story, Savvy. Now the whole campground will have nightmares." She's been a little unenthusiastic about the plan from the beginning, mostly because she wanted to hang out with her boyfriend, Ryan, but at least she's helped.

"Now," I say, "how about we try to contact Blackbeard's ghost?"

There's an enthusiastic *yes, please* from my adoring fans, so I pull the Star Board out of my bag and set it up on the table. "Everyone stand around in a circle. Frankie, please make the circle tighter."

"What is that?" Alex asks. He reaches out to touch the board, but I pull it back.

"This is a Star Board. My grandfather made it. It helps us communicate with friendly ghosts, like a Ouija board, only with stars and a special code. We're pretty sure we can talk to Blackbeard himself. You'll see. Now I need three volunteers."

Everyone raises their hands, as expected. I choose Peter, Kate, and Jolene, as planned. The four of us place our fingers on the paddle. "Who has the first question?"

A little girl raises her hand. She's probably Jolene's age. "Let's ask Blackbeard where his treasure is!"

"Why would he tell us that?" Peter asks. "He haunts this island to scare people away from it." I give Peter a small smile. He's gotten much better at embellishing the truth.

The little girl crosses her arms. "But that's the only exciting question. What else would we ask him if not about treasure?"

She's a kid after my own heart.

"What if we ask him where his body floated off to?" an older boy asks.

"Ew!" Jolene squeals, and shoves her hands into her pockets. "No way!"

"All right, enough." Frankie claps her hands and stands back. She starts shooing everyone away from the table. "Thank you, everyone, for coming. Next show is at three."

"But you said the price included a séance!" protested the boy who was curious about the location of Blackbeard's body. "You can't go back on your word or we get our money back."

"Frankie," I shout, "you're not in charge." I don't mean to sound so bossy, but we're getting nine bucks out of this. Nine bucks that I plan on giving to Mom and Dad to help with bills. We can't refund their money. "Everyone, calm down. I know what we can ask that has nothing to do with treasure or missing bodies."

Frankie returns to the circle and I clear my throat. "Edward, tell us where your ship, the *Queen Anne's Revenge*, is located." This is the question we've been trying to find the answer to for days. For real.

The same boy challenges me again. "You said his ship was called the *Adventure*." He just doesn't stop.

"He had two ships during his career," I explain. "The *Adventure* was taken here at Ocracoke when he died, but his first ship, the *Queen Anne,* sank and was never found."

"What's so important about that one?" the boy asks.

"What's your name?" I ask him.

"Darren."

"Well, Darren, let me explain something to you. No treasure was found on the *Adventure*. So if Blackbeard had any, and there's no proof that he did, but if he did, it likely went down with the *Queen Anne*."

"But how will you get to an entire ship at the bottom of the ocean?" the little girl asks.

Kate saves me. "Let's just ask the question," she says.

We all refocus on the paddle and I repeat the question. "Edward, sir, can you please tell us where the *Queen Anne* went down?"

The paddle begins to move. But not in the direction I was planning on moving it. I look at Peter, silently questioning him, but he shrugs and shakes his head. Jolene writes down each constellation the paddle visits and begins transcribing the message just as I taught her. When she's all done, it's not a location.

It's more like a warning.

ASTORMBREWS

Back at the Helm

"I want my money back!"

"What kind of answer is that?"

"This game is rigged."

My audience isn't pleased. Everyone stands up, brushing off sand and chattering about how they got ripped off. We have to refund three of them to make them happy.

And they don't even realize they got a real message from a real ghost!

Frankie gets a head start home while we pack up the Star Board.

"Sav," Kate asks. "What does it mean?"

"I don't know." I stare at the words: "A storm brews."

"Doesn't seem like it means anything." Peter tosses a stone into the bushes. "It seems unfinished."

"I think we need to know *who* the ghost is first, right, Savvy?" Kate asks.

Peter nods. "Good point. If we knew for sure who it was, it might help us figure out what they mean."

"I think it's Grandpa," Jolene says.

I shake my head. "No. It doesn't sound like Grandpa."

"How can you tell?" Peter asks. "You only get, like, three words at a time."

"I can just tell." But it's really just a feeling I have. Grandpa's been communicating through the map and clues he left behind for us before he died a month ago. The ghost is someone else. I've always thought it was Blackbeard, but this message is so different.

"Sorry to ditch, everyone, but I have to get back home," Kate says. "This was super fun. Can't wait to do it again next weekend! I'll see you at school tomorrow!" We all say goodbye and she skips off down the street.

I haven't told her about all the secrets of the treasure hunt Grandpa created. She doesn't know about the map of Ocracoke he left us or about how Dunmore Throop, his old business partner, has been trying to get our house. She doesn't know how he tracked me and my sisters down the night we found the key in Springer's Point Preserve. For now, only our family—and Peter's family—knows the truth. Well, and, of course, the scallywag Dunmore Throop himself, who knows way too much.

We catch up to Frankie and Peter walks with us as we head back home. I skate slow enough so that he can keep up. Halfway back to our house, his older brother, Robbie, pulls alongside in his fancy yellow car and rolls down the window. Robbie's the oldest cousin at sixteen and has a job at a restaurant near the harbor. We don't see him much.

"Get in," Robbie says. His fingers tap on the side of the car to the beat of his music. The engine is so loud he basically has to shout over it. Mom always says he likes noisy cars because he wants attention, but I think it's kind of a dumb way to get attention. "Dad is looking for you," he says to Peter.

"Why?" Peter asks. Robbie looks at me and my sisters and then back at Peter. Uncle Randy and Aunt Della still don't like that Peter spends a ton of time with us. They think we get him into too much trouble. And by "we" I mean "me."

"Dad said to pick you up. So that's what I'm doing. Get in."

Peter throws his walking stick into the back seat and waves to us out the window. "See you at school!"

Frankie drops her board and pushes off, pulling Jolene behind her. "Nice of our cousin to offer us a ride," she grumbles.

"I wouldn't ride in his car anyway," I say. "It smells like cigarettes and sweat."

For some reason Jolene finds this hilarious and giggles the rest of the way home.

Once inside we find Mom at her desk working on her latest project: a translation for someone's book. She's a language expert, which means she's always correcting our grammar. Jolene proudly hands her the six dollars we made.

"What's this?" Mom asks.

"Our part," Jolene says.

"To help with the bills until the historical registry for the house is finished," Frankie explains. "Until the grants come through."

"Girls, this is so sweet. How did you earn it?"

"By telling ghost stories." I pull the folded paper I have in my pocket and show her the story I wrote down. "I memorized it and we put on a show."

"To other kids? And you charged?"

"Yep." Jolene grins. "Smart, right?"

"Yes." Mom makes a face like she's trying to figure out if this is a good idea or not. "I suppose it is. They run ghost tours in town, why not have one just for kids." She folds the six dollar bills up and tucks them into a drawer. "It's a great start." She gives us each a hug and tells us she has to finish up her work, so we head up to the attic to hang out before dinner.

I have Grandpa's map of Ocracoke Island already spread out on our table and held down with a special piece of plastic that covers the entire map. Dad cut it for me. We can write on the plastic right on top of the map with erasable markers, and so far we've marked out where we found the key. Along with the key, which took a very long time to dig up under a big tree in the park, Grandpa left us a clue about a "window." Our next job is to figure out what window is so important that he would leave us a riddle about it. It's just a matter of thinking the way he did and eventually we'll figure it out. And I'm the best at thinking like Grandpa.

Pacing the attic, I wonder out loud, "Maybe the window Grandpa was talking about has to do with the ship—a special window on the ship itself." Some of the floorboards creak and groan under my feet as I walk. I peer out the portal window in the attic and look out to the ocean way in the distance. Somewhere out there, Blackbeard's famous ship rests at the bottom of the seafloor. I turn to Frankie. "What do you think?"

She shakes her head. "That wouldn't make any sense unless we found the clues completely out of order, which I guess is possible. But we don't even know where to look for the ship yet. The ocean is a very big place."

I rest my head against the wall. "There has to be something we're missing."

"Yeah," Jolene says. "Everything."

"Do you want to go to the library with me after school tomorrow to look for information on the *Queen Anne's Revenge*?" I ask Frankie. "We've got to start somewhere."

Frankie blows the bangs out of her face. "I told Ryan I'd go to the beach," she says. Ever since Ryan started teaching my sister how to surf over the summer, it's been hard to keep her in one place. When she sees the look on my face, she reconsiders. "Maybe for an hour, and then I have to go."

Jolene flops onto the big, overstuffed couch and lets her legs swing over the arm. "I'll help!" Our little dog, Py, short for "Pirate," jumps up and curls next to her.

"That's nice of you, but I doubt you'll be able to read the history books."

"I can still help take notes. I'm a very good note-taker," Jolene says. "Just tell me what to write and how to spell it."

That's not much of a help, but it's all I got. "Deal." I run my hand over the smooth surface of the plastic on top of the map. "There's still something out there waiting for us; I know it."

"And 'a storm brews,'" Frankie says, laughing. "That was a good one, Savvy."

"I didn't make that up," I say. "I swear it!"

"But 'a storm brews' doesn't make any sense."

"More proof that I didn't do it!"

Frankie's quiet. She tugs on her hair a little bit, as she always does when she's thinking. I'm beginning to wonder if she's going to help or not from here on out. She's constantly distracted and always wants to be with Ryan.

"If you don't want to do this anymore," I say, "I can swear in Kate."

"She's not a Dare sister!" Jolene says. "She doesn't even have a pirate name."

"Don't be so rude," I say. "Besides, it's not like Frankie is acting like one. And I need help. We can't do this all by ourselves."

"I didn't say I wasn't going to help." Frankie stands up. "Everything just doesn't need to be so urgent, Savannah. We have other things to worry about."

"Like what?"

"School, friends, helping with the house."

"This is helping with the house. Finding the treasure is just more proof that Grandpa was right all along and that his artifacts and everything are worth being in the historical registry."

"I know that. I'm just not as obsessed as you, I guess."

"I'm not obsessed. I'm focused."

Frankie throws her hands up in the air. "Whatever." She begins to head downstairs. "I'll help you for an hour tomorrow but that's it."

"Fine."

"Fine."

Jolene closes her eyes and sighs. "I'm working with such unprofessors."

"I think you mean unprofessionals."

"That's what I said."

A Scallywag's Return

At lunch on Monday, I race out to the picnic tables to meet Kate and Peter. It's a sunny, warm fall day and, most important, my twelfth birthday. I decide to tell everyone the story of Dunmore Throop and what happened the night he chased us in the woods. Since not a lot happens in Ocracoke other than vacationing families with their loud parties and leftover trash, it's all anyone has talked about for days. But despite all the rumors, no one really knows what happened.

Except us.

I tell the truth of most of that night, but I say we're not sure what he was after, only that we know it was something that belonged to Grandpa. I don't want anyone to know we have a key in our house that might have belonged to Blackbeard himself.

Ashley, one of Frankie's friends, asks, "Do you think Throop's going to come back and try again?"

"He might," I say. "We have to keep a good lookout at all times."

"I don't think it's likely," Frankie says. "Uncle Randy scared him off, calling the sheriff and all."

"Yeah, but if he still thinks there's treasure in your house," Peter mumbles. "I'm just saying . . ."

I can't believe he lets that slip. I kick him under the table.

"Ouch!"

"You have treasure in your house?" Frankie's surfer boyfriend, Ryan, asks her.

"Well, not exactly," Frankie starts to explain. "But . . ."

"Yes, we do!" Jolene shouts. "It's full of Grandpa's treasures." She means all the artifacts Grandpa found throughout his life. All of which are awesome, and treasures to us, but not treasure like the others are thinking. And yet Throop was after something in our house as well; it was the reason he wanted to buy the house. Somehow it all comes together, but I just haven't figured it out yet.

Frankie leads her friends off to go do their own thing. I think she's a little embarrassed since they don't seem to totally believe what we're saying.

"Happy Birthday, Sav!" Ryan calls back to me as they go. I wish he wouldn't be nice to me; it makes it harder for me to be angry that he's stealing my sister.

"Savannah, are you going to eat that?" Peter points to my pudding cup. I slide it across the table to him. It's the least I can do for him after he basically saved our lives on the beach by running for our parents the night Throop was after us. Peter used to annoy me because he'd get me into trouble all the time, but he's gotten a lot better. I suppose we should come up with a pirate name for him like we did for ourselves.

After school, Kate wants me to teach her some tricks on the skateboard. I'd rather rush to the library, but Frankie is nowhere in sight. I also want to be a better friend, because I really missed Kate when we weren't talking, so I show her a couple of things. "I'm not the best at this, but it's called an ollie."

I hop on the skateboard, roll a bit, and jump with it, shifting my weight just right so that the board stays up with me and I land back down on it. I'm a bit wobbly but it's not my worst.

"That's so cool!" she says. "How did you learn that?"

"Frankie."

"I wish I had a big sister. So much better than an older brother who pretends I don't exist."

"I guess." Frankie's only half here most of the time and not showing up at all right now even though she promised she'd help for an hour. It makes me want to tell Kate everything about the treasure map, about the clues Grandpa left us, and the key, and the fact there's something more out there. But I made my sisters swear to secrecy, so I can't break my own oath. "I'm going to go to the library now. Do you want to come?"

"What do you have to do there?"

"I want to read some about Blackbeard's ships. Boring, I guess. It's okay if you don't."

"No, I'll help. It's your birthday! It'll be my gift." She grins and her new braces sparkle in the sun.

"Okay, cool."

I flip up my board and hand it to Kate to practice riding and keeping her balance as we walk to the library.

"Hey!" Jolene yells behind us. "Wait for me!" She runs to catch up, her sneakers kicking up sand as she moves. "I told you I wanted to go with you."

I quietly groan, but I did tell her she could take notes even though this whole thing would go a whole lot faster without her. "Hurry up then."

The three of us enter the library and say hi to Mr. Brown as we pass his desk. He's been the librarian since before I was born and always lets me renew books as many times as I want.

He looks up from his newspaper as we pass by. "Afternoon, ladies. Anything I can help you with?"

"No thank you, sir. I've got it." I lead the way to the card catalog, a giant cupboard of little drawers that have note cards that list every single book in the library. Every book is coded with a number, and then you find that number on the shelves to find the book. It's kind of like some of the codes Grandpa made up, so I guess that's why I like it so much.

I search under "B" for Blackbeard and find three books about pirates. Jolene copies the names and numbers down on a note card with a tiny pencil, which takes ridiculously long but makes her feel important. Then we make our way to the back of the library.

Kate finds the first one, a really old book by somebody Hort, and pulls it off the shelf. I find another old one by a guy named Howard Pyle and a newer one by the Marine Research Society. I hand that one to Jolene. "Do you know how to use the index?" I ask her. She shakes her head, so I flip to the back of the book and show her the long list of subjects. "You look under the letter of the subject you want. We want 'Q' for *Queen Anne's Revenge*. You can find 'queen,' right?"

Jolene flips to "Q" and points to it. Then she finds the ship's name and the number next to it. "That's the page it's on?" she asks.

"Yep. You got it!"

The three of us search our books for more information and diagrams, and then I trade with Kate and then Jolene to go through hers because she can't read well enough yet. But I don't find anything that seems very important. Definitely nothing that talks about a window. I decide to copy the pages so I can take them home and look at them more closely again later.

"What exactly do you want to find out?" Kate asks.

"I'm not sure," I admit. "Anything that might show why Throop was so interested in a ship that's never been found. I mean, what's on it that he wants it so bad?"

"Pirate treasure, I'm sure."

"I don't know." I don't say anything else to her, but Grandpa always seemed sure he'd find the treasure here on Ocracoke Island. I reach up for the ring necklace Dad made for me after Grandpa died. The celestial ring on it looks like a regular ring until you unfold it, and then it has more rings inside with symbols all over them. Dad said that it was used for navigation and that Grandpa gave it to him when he was young. The celestial ring was one of the few things Grandpa never showed me or talked about when he was alive. I only found out about it when Dad made it into a necklace for me. I wonder what else he had that I never knew about. What else might be hiding in my house. "You'd think there'd be more books on pirates."

"Maybe when you get older, you'll have to write your own," Kate says. "Like your mom. You already write great ghost stories."

"Thanks! I think I'd rather hunt for treasure than write about it, but you never know. Well, I guess that's it for today," I say, and set the books on the reshelving table. "Thanks for your help."

"Sure." She smiles back at me. "It's the least I can do

for your showing me those tricks. Can you teach me more tomorrow?"

"Sure!" I say. We head outside and walk partway home together, until we get to Kate's street and say goodbye. Jolene sits on her skateboard and holds the rope so I can pull her home.

"Savvy?" Jolene asks quietly, as I push off in the sandy street.

"Yeah?"

She drags a small twig on the sandy road, leaving a little trail behind us as we move. "What was the other riddle Grandpa used to always say? There was the elbow one, the window one, and what's the third?"

I only need to think about it for a second. "Something about the word 'short,' " I answer. "What five-letter word becomes shorter when you add two letters?" Sometimes I used to get tired of hearing him say them over and over. I mean, a riddle isn't a riddle once you know the answer, but he'd quiz us all the time and thought it was hilarious. Now I realize he was sort of training us, preparing us for these clues, and I'd give anything to have him quiz me one last time.

"Elbow, window, short," Jolene repeats a few times, playing around with the words in her mouth like they might make sense the more she says them. "Elbow, window, short."

"Doesn't make sense to me either," I say.

"Do you think 'short' is a clue like the other two riddles?"

"I guess it could be." I'm worried we'll never find the connection to any of them and that's the only way to get closer to the *Queen Anne's Revenge*. And whatever the key unlocks. If "short" is an answer to a clue we haven't found yet, then we have two dead ends. Happy Birthday to me.

When we come around the bend to our house, there's a fancy black car in the driveway. I skid my board to a stop and Jolene rolls right into my ankles.

"Ow!"

"Sorry! You didn't give a warning!" She jumps off her board and rubs the back of my legs.

I swat her away. "It's fine!"

"Whose car is that?" she asks.

"I don't know. Let's go find out." We prop our boards up on the porch and go inside. In the kitchen there's a strange man talking to our mom. At first, I think it might be Throop, and my legs get wobbly. I never want to run into him again. But this man sounds local and Throop wasn't from here. We hide around the corner and listen.

Mom signs a piece of paper and hands it back to the man. He hands her a big envelope of papers. "Thank you, ma'am. If you have any questions, you can call the courthouse in Manteo." He nods a goodbye and lets himself out the door, walking right past us in the hall as if we're invisible. Once we hear his car start, we go into the kitchen. Mom looks tired as she flips through the packet of papers the man left behind.

"Who was that?" I ask.

"Someone delivering important papers," she says, looking at us like she's sorry about something.

"For what?" Jolene asks.

"Dunmore Throop is taking us to court."

A Mysterious New Crewmate

At dinner, for which I chose lasagna since it's my birthday, everyone talks at once. Mom and Dad discuss the paperwork they received and I interrogate Frankie about why she didn't show up at the library.

"I got stuck after school with Ashley and Dawn working on a project we have to do for history," she says. "Geez, Sav, there are other things going on in the world besides your treasure hunt."

"*My* treasure hunt? I thought we were all doing this together?"

There's a splat and a shriek from the kitchen. "That's my dinner!" Jolene yells at Py for stealing her lasagna that she dropped onto the floor.

Everyone is upset and getting louder by the second and it's basically the worst birthday dinner ever, until

Dad yells the loudest. "All right, everyone just quiet down for one minute so I can think!"

We all stare at him. Dad hardly ever shouts. Going to court must be serious.

Jolene drops her head. "Sorry, Daddy."

"It's okay. I didn't mean to be so loud," Dad sighs. "Go ahead and get yourself a new piece and please be careful this time."

Jolene carefully scoops a new piece of lasagna onto her plate and gets back to her chair without losing her dinner a second time. I'm tempted to tell her it might be easier to see if she took off the eye patch but I know that won't change her mind about wearing it.

"Are you going to tell us what this court thing is even about?" Frankie stabs her lasagna with a fork. "Why is Throop suing us? Why can't he just leave us alone?"

Dad wipes his mouth with a napkin. "That's a really good question that I'm not entirely sure I know the answer to. Other than to say he still believes this house belongs to him and now, since he can't buy it, he's going to fight us in court for it. And if this doesn't come to an end soon, I'm not sure how much longer I can do this." I envision Dad and Throop in an epic sword battle and almost say that out loud. But Dad rubs his eyes and frowns, so I don't say anything. He's been really sad since Grandpa died. I miss his big smile and goofy jokes.

Mom squeezes Dad's hand and then passes the salad to Frankie. "But we don't want you girls to worry. Your dad and I will figure it all out. Uncle Randy has a lawyer friend for us to talk to."

"We want you to focus on school," Dad says.

"And the treasure hunt!" Jolene says.

Dad looks at Jolene, uncertain. "Sure." He gently squeezes Frankie's arm and looks at me. "Let the adults take care of this part. You have nothing to worry about."

Frankie doesn't look completely convinced, and neither am I, but she says nothing else and goes back to murdering her lasagna.

I watch Mom and Dad give each other strange looks. Even though Mom always says no secrets, I can tell they're keeping one.

After we clean up dinner, Mom tells us to finish our homework and we'll do cake and presents shortly. We head up to the attic and stare at Grandpa's map instead.

"Now what?" I ask no one in particular as I search the map for more clues.

Frankie drops onto the couch, and dust flies up in the air. "Now we just have to hope Mom and Dad know what they're doing."

I shake my head. "I can't just sit and watch and do nothing. We have to figure out this window clue."

"I don't know if it matters now, Savvy."

"Of course it matters. It matters more than ever." I circle Teach's Hole, which is the spot where Blackbeard died, in the water not far from the beach at Springer's Point. Then I draw a line from Springer's Point, where we found the key, to our house and circle our house. These are the only important spots I know so far. Where on the island is a window? A special window or a big window or a famous window?

"What if the window isn't an actual window at all?" I ask my sisters. "Grandpa's first clue was about an elbow, but not a real elbow." He meant a bend in a branch of the Elbow Tree, a giant, gnarly live oak tree in the park.

"Then I'm totally lost," Frankie says.

Jolene pulls up her eye patch. "I'm the lostest."

We have no answers. I don't even bring up the possibility of "short" being a clue. Jolene disappears downstairs to watch TV. Frankie pulls out her homework and I do the same even though I can't concentrate. I'm supposed to write a three-paragraph essay about what I did over the summer, which was mostly help take care of Grandpa when he got sick. The last couple of months he was with us, he barely recognized us anymore. I don't really want to write about that. All my friends will have essays about fun things they did at the beach and the park, fishing and sailing, helping at their parents' shops. My summer wasn't so fun until we got the special coded message and treasure map from Grandpa after the funeral, but I can't write about that either.

"Savvy," Frankie says, "please stop tapping your pencil."

"Sorry." I push my notebook away and stand up. "I'm going to sit on the porch for a while."

Outside it's warm and muggy but I kind of like it.

The sun is below the horizon but there's enough dusky light to still see most everything. Swinging on the porch swing reminds me of sitting out here after dinner with Grandpa and my sisters. We'd take a walk after dinner and then sometimes Mom and Dad would join us with iced tea and sugar cookies. We'd listen to the evening birds, tree frogs, and katydids, and Grandpa would tell stories about his adventures. Ever since he got sick, we haven't spent any time as a family on the porch, or much of anywhere, to be honest. Meals, but that's about it. Maybe I'll just write about last year's summer instead.

I light one of the candles meant to keep flies away. It doesn't work very well but I like the flickering flame and citrus smell. I hear something scuffling in a bush in a shadowy area of the yard. Probably a squirrel or bird. But I hear squirrels and birds all the time and this is louder.

Peering over the railing, I strain to see what's causing the noise, a little afraid it might be Dunmore Throop. The thought makes me want to run, but instead I say, "Hello? Who's out there?"

Up pops a curly head of blond-gray hair and giant hot-pink sunglasses, which match her dress. Ms. Carolina Davis. Our neighbor whom we hardly see.

"Ms. Davis, can I help you with something?"

"Oh darlin'. I'm trying to find my cat Casper and I dropped my flashlight over the fence into your bushes. Sorry to disturb you!" She lowers her sunglasses for just a second, but I can't get a good look at her eyes. It's too dark out now and I have no idea how she can see anything with them on. "Would you be a dear and see if you can crawl under here and fetch it for me?"

"Sure, ma'am," I say, and hop down the steps. Ms. Davis has always been a very private neighbor. She's hardly talked to us and is never without her giant sunglasses, even in the middle of the night. Frankie and I always joke that she's a retired celebrity hiding out in Ocracoke.

I crawl under the bush, feeling around the sand until my hand touches hard plastic. "There you go."

She smiles when I give it to her. "Did you know before your family moved in, your grandpa and I used to sit on that porch together on nights like this and play Scrabble?"

"What?" Grandpa and Carolina Davis were close friends? This was news to me.

"Yes, we did. He told me all kinds of unbelievable stories about his travels. I'd bring lemonade. He'd smoke that pipe with the cherry tobacco." She smiles again and looks away. At least, I think she looks away; it's hard to tell with those dark glasses. "I miss talking to that man."

Me too, I think. "Why'd you stop?"

"Well, when your family moved in, he got the company he truly wanted, I'm sure. We still talked from time to time, but as you girls got older, I think he enjoyed your company more."

"I'm sorry."

"Don't be! C'est la vie!" She swats at nothing. "I've wasted the last few years hiding out in my house, not getting to know my own neighbors, but not anymore."

"It's very nice to officially meet you," I say.

"Oh, and I keep meaning to tell your father: I have a few of your grandfather's books in my house. He was always lending me enormous volumes of things I could never get through."

"Sounds like Grandpa," I say.

"I'll bring them over soon. Thank you for your help—Savannah, is that right?"

"Yes, ma'am. And no hurry."

"Cornelius had a special place in his heart for you." She gently taps my nose. "Ever since you were a tiny baby, he used to say that your light shone brighter than the lighthouse. Such an expressive face you have."

"Thank you?" If I have any expression on my face right now it's because Ms. Davis is making me feel a little awkward. I pull away from her and start back toward the porch. "Good night, ma'am."

"Sleep tight! Now I've got to get back to finding that darn cat!" She turns and shines her light under the porch, where two bright yellow eyes shine back. As I leave, I hear her calling "here kitty-kitty!"

When I open the door to go back inside, Mom, Dad, Frankie, and Jolene are standing right in the hall. Mom has a small chocolate cake lit with twelve candles. They all start singing.

"Happy Birthday, my little tiger shark," Dad says, and hugs me tight. "I'm sorry we've all been so distracted tonight. But we got you something special." He reaches around to the table and hands me a big, brightly wrapped box.

We sit in the living room and I open the box. Inside is a model of a clipper ship, which is one of the biggest pirate ships. They have huge sails and carry hundreds of people.

"You can put that together yourself," Dad says. "Do you like it?"

"Yes! It looks hard, though," I say, examining the box. There seem to be thousands of pieces.

Dad sits next to me. "I used to do these all the time when I was your age. It's like putting together a puzzle, you just do it bit by bit. I'll help you with it."

"Okay, cool!"

Mom gathers us for cake in the kitchen. "We thought it would make up for the wooden ship Grandpa carved and said he'd give you when you turned twelve."

"Oh yeah," I say. "Frankie and I were talking about that a while ago, about how I was so fascinated by it and I'd fall asleep in his office watching him carve it when I was little. We wondered whatever happened to it." Thinking about that little ship makes me feel raw all over again. I loved watching Grandpa whether he was carving, writing, drawing maps, or even smoking his pipe.

Dad shrugs. "No idea. For all we know it's lost somewhere in this house. There's definitely plenty of hiding places. I'm sure it will turn up someday. But for now, you have one to build yourself."

Jolene holds up a fork. "And chocolate cake!"

A Ghost of an Idea

All night long I think about what Ms. Davis told me Grandpa said about me. It makes me miss him so much more and I don't sleep well. I keep having a dream that Grandpa is walking on the beach and no matter how fast I run, I can't catch up to him. Way in the distance is a huge clipper ship and I have the feeling that's where Grandpa is headed. But every time I call his name, he looks over his shoulder like he can hear me but he can't see me.

All my muscles are tight the next morning. I lie in bed for a few extra minutes rolling the celestial ring between my fingers and trying to think like Grandpa. But like my dream, I don't know if I'll ever catch up to him.

On the walk to school, I don't even skate, I just carry my board and think, *Elbow, window, short.*

"What's wrong with you?" Frankie skates slow to keep pace with me as she tows Jolene behind her.

"Just a lot to think about."

"Did you think about finishing your homework?"

"No. And stop trying to be Mom."

"I'm not trying to be Mom, but school just started and you've already missed so many days." She leans in toward me and whispers, even though no one is around, "Because you were digging in the park to find the key."

"I won't have any trouble catching up." Which is true. We're only a little over a month into school anyway and so far it's mostly a repeat of last year. Grandpa used to tease me that I have a photographic memory. I don't remember *everything* but I do remember all the fractions I learned last year and I'm positive I don't need to practice again. So Frankie can take her homework and—

"There's another festival soon?" Jolene suddenly asks from behind us. She jumps off her board and walks over to a telephone pole where a flyer has been posted. She lifts the eye patch so she can see the poster better. It looks like it has a picture of the lighthouse on it.

"I don't think so," Frankie says. "Not until the Fall Festival."

"Something's happening." Jolene shrugs. "Banana . . . light . . ." she tries to read.

"That's 'biannual,'" Frankie reads it for her. "'Biannual Cleaning at the Lighthouse.' They're looking for volunteers to help clean up the grounds when they go up to wash the lens."

"Why do they have to clean the lens anyway?"

"To make sure everything is in working order. It's still an important lighthouse and needs to be bright for boats way out in the ocean."

"And also so the ghost of Theodosia can see better," I say, thinking that is definitely going to be the next story I charge the campground kids to listen to.

Jolene mimes looking through a telescope. "I wish we could climb up it and look out over all the land."

"It's not that tall," I say. "The one in Hatteras is way better."

"You're grumpy this morning. You turn twelve and suddenly know everything." Frankie steps back on her board. "Come on, Jolene, I'll pull you the rest of the way."

I sigh and watch my sisters roll ahead of me. I am grumpy. A couple of kids run past me, and sand sprays from under their shoes and hits me. "Hey!" I shout as they reach the school and I drag myself in the door, not looking forward to another day of relearning things.

But it turns out, I do learn something new. At the end of the day, in science, Mr. Baranski brings up the lighthouse cleaning. "Those of you who want to join me at the cleanup in a couple of weeks, I'll be assisting the rangers in some native plantings. Could mean some extra credit for those who need it." He looks right at Peter.

"Are they going to let us go up to the top this time?" Peter asks. "'Cause I'll definitely do that for extra credit."

"No," Mr. Baranski says. "I don't know that it will ever be restored enough for that. They've repaired the lens and windows over the years, but apparently the spiral stairs can't take too much traffic."

"It doesn't make sense we can't even go inside our own lighthouse." Peter has always wanted to climb to the top, just like Jolene, and look out over the ocean.

"Yeah," other kids agree. "We should be allowed."

"They obviously go up to fix the light and stuff, so it has to be safe."

"I guess just not safe enough for a bunch of wily fifth and sixth graders. But anyway, back to botany." Mr. Baranski writes down the names of native plants he'll be helping with, but my brain has gone somewhere else, putting together a different puzzle.

The lighthouse cleaning is scheduled for the same weekend every year. Grandpa would know that. Grandpa was also in the navy, and the lighthouse has been taken care of by the Coast Guard for a long time, which means if anyone would have had the contacts to get in there to hide something important, it was Grandpa.

On top of that, the lighthouse is over a hundred years old. So that means all its parts are too, including the windows. That would make for a unique window on the island. Probably the oldest.

Probably the window in Grandpa's riddle, the one he wants me to find.

Means to an End

After school, Kate wants me to teach her some more skateboarding tricks. "My mom said if I was going to keep practicing, I had to get a helmet." She pulls out of her backpack a bright blue helmet with a huge white daisy on both sides and straps it on. Her two brown braids hang down over each shoulder. It's much cuter than the plain black one I wear.

"Looks good!" I try to sound cheerful and excited, but I can't stop thinking about checking out the lighthouse on the way home. But we ride to the school playground, Jolene in tow, and I teach both of them some more balancing tricks.

"You're going to have to get your own board soon so we can all skate together," I tell Kate. "We might have an old one of Frankie's you can use until you get your own. She won't care. Want to come over and look?"

"Sure!"

"I just want to go over to the lighthouse first, if it's okay," I say. "Something I need to look at."

Kate puts her helmet back into her bag. "No problem."

Jolene groans. "I'm hungry. That's the long way."

"Then you go the regular way," I tell her.

She crosses her arms. "I'm not supposed to walk home by myself."

I look back at the bike rack near the school, but Dad has already left for the day too, which is kind of strange because he usually stays later than us to help students after class. Who knows where Frankie is. I'm going to have to start carrying walkie-talkies just to find her.

"Looks like you're stuck with us then," I say. "We'll walk and you can practice your traveling."

This seems to make her happy. Jolene salutes me, drops her board, and pushes off with one foot, nearly landing on her butt. I grab her arm before she wipes out.

Kate helps to steady her. "Good reflexes," she says to me, and we cross over to the next street and head toward the lighthouse. Despite almost falling, Jolene actually does a great job getting herself the rest of the way there without injury.

A couple of people are walking around the little boardwalk beneath the lighthouse when we get there, taking pictures. Jolene and I drop our boards and we all leave our bookbags by the fence where people park their bikes.

The lighthouse is seventy-five feet tall and pure

white. Next to it is the old lighthouse keeper's house, with a bright red metal roof and large screened-in porch. It's the oldest house on the island, but no one lives in it anymore. Now everything is electric and people just come in occasionally to clean everything.

We walk around the base and I examine the heavy padlock on the door. Grandpa taught me a lot of cool things, like codes and knots, but he never taught me how to pick a lock.

"What did you want to look at exactly?" Kate asks.

I tell her part of the truth even though it probably sounds ridiculous. "When Mr. Baranski was talking about the lighthouse, I was thinking about how old it is, how old all the parts are, like the door. And windows."

Jolene looks up at me, her one unpatched eye wide. "What ancient invention allowed people to see through walls?" she whispers.

"Or through storms," I say.

"A storm brews," Jolene whispers, and takes my hand.

Kate looks at us funny. "What are you two talking about?"

"Nothing," I say, squeezing Jolene's hand. "Just some funny riddles our grandpa used to tell us." Jolene squeezes back.

Kate doesn't seem bothered by our coded conversation. "Your grandpa was so cool. Remember that time in third grade when he came in to talk to the class for career day about making maps?"

"Oh yeah . . . I forgot about that," I say. We start walking back to our boards and bags and I'm only half listening to Kate as I also strategize how I'm going to get inside the lighthouse on the day of the cleaning.

"I'll never forget how he said some day maps would no longer be on paper, and some day he wouldn't have a job. He said the art of making maps would be lost because they'd be electronic or something and everyone could just type in where they wanted to go."

"That's silly," Jolene says. "How would you take an electric map with you on a trip?"

Kate slings her backpack up on her shoulder. "He had some idea that it would fit in your pocket."

"Grandpa was full of interesting ideas," I say, rolling the celestial ring between my fingers. Grandpa also said that the art of making maps was already mostly lost but that he still enjoyed making them. He often remade maps that already existed, like the treasure map of Ocracoke in our attic.

"What's the point of making a map that already exists?" I asked him one day when he was working at the kitchen table with fancy inks and paper.

"Sometimes the only point is the thing itself," he told me. "Sometimes the means is the end."

I had no idea what he meant by that. Still don't.

Before we leave, Jolene says, "So we're going to have to come back sometime, right, Savvy?" I nod but don't say anything else. I really want to tell Kate everything, but I'm not sure I should.

When we get home, Jolene runs up to the porch and yells, "Finally, I can eat!" As if we'd been gone for days.

I lead Kate to the shed to search for Frankie's old skateboard. It takes only a little digging to find it.

"Wow," she says, turning the board over in her hands. "You're sure Frankie won't mind?"

I shake my head. "Do you see how dirty that is? I don't think she even remembers she has it."

"Can I put stickers on it like yours?"

I grin. "Yes! It's yours now. I have some extras to get you started." It's so nice being friends again. I know if I keep holding on to this secret, though, it's going to get in the way. Eventually I'm going to have to tell Kate the truth about the Dare family legacy.

Secret Keeper

Since I can't do much until the lighthouse cleanup weekend, I figure I'll pass the time planning our next ghost story event. There probably won't be a big crowd of vacationers this late in the season but there's always some.

After school each day, Kate, Jolene, and I practice tricks for an hour at the playground and then go home and sit on the Queen Mary's porch to write our next script. We have so much fun coming up with ghost stories I even forget about the treasure hunt a little bit. It sort of feels like last year, before Grandpa died, before Kate and I had our big fight and I pushed her into a garbage can, before I ever laid eyes on creepy Dunmore Throop. I keep hoping Frankie will join us, but most of the time she's with Ryan.

But one afternoon she comes storming up the steps

of the porch. Her face is red and sweaty like she just ran all the way home from school.

"You all right, Frankie?" I ask before she opens the door to the house.

"I'm fine." She blows her bangs out of her face, looks at our lemonade and notebooks for a second, and then stomps inside.

"Boy problems?" Kate whispers.

Jolene sighs. "Boys are always problems," she says, trying to sound grown-up and wise.

Kate and I crack up. "So true, Jolene," Kate says. "So true."

"So back to this." I tap the paper with my pencil. "Let's do the story about Theodosia. We can pretend to contact her and talk about where she went when she disappeared? People would love something like that, don't you think?"

"Or maybe we talk to the sailor she's supposedly trying to find?" Kate suggests.

"I like that idea too. Keeps her mysterious." I write down "missing sailor." "Let's give him a name."

"Brandon," Jolene says immediately.

"Brandon?" I laugh. "Where'd you come up with that?"

"It just sounds good." She clasps her hands together and gives her voice an airy sound. "Brandon and Theodosia, star-cropped lovers, just like Frankie and Ryan."

"I think you mean star-*crossed*," Kate says.

"That's what I said."

"All right." I write down his name. "So we'll pretend we're trying to talk to Theodosia, but really . . . Brandon will make an appearance and he'll say something like 'stay away from the beaches lest you suffer the same fate as my beloved Theodosia' . . ." I stop myself and scratch it out. "No, that will take way too long with the Star Board."

Kate looks at her watch. "Oh! I'm sorry I can't help you more," she says. "My mom said if I didn't clean my room today, she was packing up all my stuff and donating it to Goodwill." She hugs us both goodbye. "See you tomorrow at the campground!"

Kate jumps down the steps and rides off on her skateboard. Once she's long gone, Jolene says, "It's hard keeping secrets from Kate. I like her."

"Me too." I gather up our paper and pencils. "Come on. Let's find out what's wrong with Frankie."

We walk into the kitchen, where Frankie and Mom are talking. They stop as soon as they see us. "Hi, girls," Mom says. "Hungry for a snack?"

Frankie rubs her face, announces she's taking a shower, and leaves the room.

"Is Frankie mad at me?" I ask Mom.

"Oh no, darling."

"Is she mad at me?" Jolene asks.

"Of course not. Who could ever get mad at a cherub like you?"

Me, for one, but I don't say that out loud.

"Don't worry, girls. She'll be just fine."

I'm about to ask what her problem is when Dad comes in. He has a large yellow envelope and says, "We have an official court date. October twenty-ninth." He looks up from his papers. "Oh, hi, girls. How was school?"

"Boring," I say. "Dad, what's going to happen when you go to court?"

"I'm not completely sure, Savvy. I'm hoping it won't come to that."

"We haven't been able to find the deed to the house," Mom says. "But when we do, that should settle everything."

"What's a deed?" Jolene asks.

"A deed proves who owns the house. If we can find it, we at least have proof of Grandpa and Grandma's ownership, which will help our case. But it seems to have disappeared off the map. The town doesn't even have a copy." Mom forces a smile. "Dad and I are on our own treasure hunt now!"

Part of me wants to tell them what I think is the next step in *our* treasure hunt: climbing the lighthouse. Mom and Dad said we could continue the hunt, but after what happened with Throop on the beach, they made us promise to let them know where we were. But if I mention climbing the lighthouse, I know they will forbid it.

I can feel Jolene staring at me. She's probably thinking the same thing.

A Ghostly Message

That night after dinner, I ask Frankie if she'll join us in the attic for a meeting. "There's something I need to ask the ghost and I think it works best with all three of us."

Frankie plops into the overstuffed chair; her long legs hang over one side, and her head hangs over the other. She drapes an arm over her face. I want to ask her what happened at school today, but from the looks of it, she's not going to talk about it.

Jolene goes right to the dress-up trunk and pulls on one of her princess dresses and the giant feathered pirate hat Frankie used to wear. She brings me a pair of satiny red-and-black-striped pants and a huge poofy-sleeved shirt. She speaks with a not-so-bad British accent. "Frances, do you want to wear the skirt with the suspenders?"

Frankie gives Jolene the big-sister look of death. "Do not call me that."

Jolene shrugs as if Frankie didn't say anything at all and drops them back into the box. "I guess that's a no."

I slide out the Star Board and set it up. Frankie lights a candle, so at least she's partially involved. The three of us sit cross-legged around the board and after saying a few nice things to encourage the ghost to visit us, I ask my question. "Mr. Teach, is the lighthouse window important?"

The room is quiet except for an occasional twig falling on the metal roof.

"You know"—Frankie looks at me—"we don't know for sure we're even talking to Blackbeard's ghost. What if it's someone else?"

"Like who? They've been talking to us for weeks," I say. "And everything has helped us so far, so it has to be Blackbeard." I repeat my question, adding, "You've been so helpful, sir. If you could please talk to us again, we'd be eternally grateful."

But nothing happens.

"What are you planning, Savannah?" Frankie asks.

"What do you mean?"

"I mean, why this question about the lighthouse? What are you planning?"

"She's going up to the top!" Jolene says. "That's the important window from Grandpa's riddle."

Now *I* get the big-sister look of death. "How in

the world are you going to do that? It's locked all the time."

"I'm going to sneak in next weekend during the cleanup. You can both be lookouts and I'll hurry in when they unlock the door."

Frankie shakes her head like I'm ridiculous. "Rangers will be at the lighthouse. And Coast Guard. They'll see you."

"I'll be fast. And very quiet."

"Never going to work." Frankie leans back against the chair and closes her eyes. I can tell she's done with the Star Board.

"Do you have a better idea? We've got nothing else to go by!"

Jolene watches us as if we're a tennis match. Frankie stands up and dusts herself off as though she was outside sitting in the dirt, like she's trying to rid herself of everything in the attic once and for all. "No. I'm out of ideas. We don't have enough clues from Grandpa. This has gotten too complicated."

It's not like my big sister to give up. I have to ask. "Last week, you were still on board. And now it's like you don't believe any of this anymore. What happened today, Frankie?"

"Nothing." She starts to leave but then turns around. "Just know that I stuck up for you and all it did was cause more trouble." She stomps down the attic stairs. I wince when I hear her bedroom door slam.

"What do you think she meant?" Jolene whispers.

I lean back on my elbows. "I have no idea." Why would Frankie have to stick up for me?

Jolene seems uncomfortable and after a minute she gets up to leave too.

"Where are you going?" I ask.

"Homework?" she says like it's a question.

"Yeah, I'm sure you have tons, first grader," I say sarcastically. "Go ahead. Go." And Jolene follows in Frankie's footsteps.

"Ugh. Grandpa, everything's falling apart," I say to the rafters. "I don't think I'll ever understand why you did this, why you didn't just tell us what to do before you died." The candle flickers a little bit. I curl up on the couch, lean against its cushiony arm, and stare at the Star Board. The light from the candle shines on it, illuminating the constellations.

The very first time I used it was with Grandpa right after he made it. I was like Jolene then, a little scared of it. He said not to be afraid, that it was only meant for fun.

"Besides, Savvy," he said. "If you're ever lucky enough to talk to a spirit, you should be grateful, not scared."

"Why?" I asked.

"Because if they choose to talk to you, you must be very special!"

"Have you ever talked to one?"

"Nah," Grandpa said. "Ghosts don't care about old

men like me. I'm not that far off from joining them! They leave their messages with the young."

"I don't know if I want any messages."

"If you don't, then they won't send you any." Grandpa spun the board to me. "Want to try?"

Nothing happened that day except Grandpa pushed the paddle around to spell "I love you." "That's cheating," I said, leaning into his soft arm.

"Maybe." Grandpa hugged me. "Maybe not."

Nothing unusual ever happened with it until everything with our house and Dunmore Throop began. Maybe Frankie's right, maybe it's not Blackbeard. Maybe it's all just a weird coincidence, maybe we all kind of made it happen every time a message was spelled out. It never mattered until we got Grandpa's map and decided to be all serious about contacting Blackbeard's ghost, which makes me think it has to be Blackbeard.

"You're gonna have to tell us something, sir, or we're never going to figure this out on our own," I plead to no one, pressing my hands on my face to stop myself from crying.

There's a scratching noise. I look back at the board.

"Hello?"

Around the room, everything seems in place; there's no sound, no smell. The air is still, even the candle flame is still. I grab a pencil and piece of paper and walk over to the board and sit in front of it, gently placing my left hand on the paddle. Slowly it begins to move under my hand. It's never done this! I can hardly breathe. As the paddle visits stars on the board, I write down each of the constellations with my free hand.

It doesn't take very long. That's one thing that's consistent with the Star Board. The messages are all short. Only three words, once I translate the constellations into letters. A tiny message only for me.

The brothers lose.

Trouble in the Ranks

"What do you think it means, Peter?" I ask my cousin at lunch the next school day. It's raining, so we have to eat in our classroom at our desks. Peter and I turn them so we face each other and hunch over our food as we quietly talk. Kate's out sick, so we don't have to worry about keeping secrets from her.

"What does Frankie think?"

"She wasn't there. I haven't told her yet."

He looks at me suspiciously and takes a big bite of his peanut butter and jelly before he answers. "Why would I know what it means?"

"Because, 'the brothers lose'? I'm sure it's about you, Robbie, and Will."

"What makes you think that?"

"Because!" I'm starting to get impatient. "You're part of this now. And you're brothers!"

"So you're saying we lose out on the treasure? Because you invited me into this whole thing, and you said we would split the reward."

"Of course we will. I would never go back on my word. That's not what I'm saying!"

Peter shrugs. "Well, then how would we lose?" He shoves the last bit of his sandwich into his mouth.

"I don't know, Peter. That's why I'm asking you what you think!"

Mrs. Erickson taps a ruler on her desk. "Savannah," she warns. "Inside voices please."

"Yes, ma'am." I lean in toward Peter a little bit. "I'm going to get inside the lighthouse next weekend." I tell Peter my entire plan for sneaking in and up to the top without being seen. He nods as I talk but when I'm done, all he says is, "I want in."

"What do you mean?"

"I've wanted to go inside that thing since I was in preschool, are you kidding? You're not going to the top without me."

My first thought is, I can't have Peter slowing me down or risking our getting caught. But then again, it would be really nice to not climb those dark, steep, spiral stairs all by myself. I wouldn't dream of bringing Jolene and I'm pretty sure Frankie won't do it, so Peter is it.

"You have to be very quick."

"I can be quick."

"And very quiet."

"I can do that too."

"And if anyone asks us any questions, you might have to lie. You'd have to pretend you don't know going to the top is illegal."

Peter looks over his apple at me, his eyes wide with fear. "It's *illegal*?"

I smack my forehead. "Yeah, dummy, that's why we're making this whole plan to sneak in."

He smirks at me and crunches a loud bite of apple. "I was kidding. Gotcha!"

I guess he can pretend pretty well after all.

"There's only one problem," he adds. "And it's a big one."

"What?"

"My dad told us last night there's a hurricane coming. He said it could mess up his fishing trip on the weekend if the weather's bad enough. And if the weather's bad, they'll probably postpone the lighthouse cleanup."

"We'll just hope it's not bad. And if it is, we'll carry out our plan on the new date." But I know we have only a couple of weeks before that court date.

At the end of the day, I head over to my dad's classroom to ask him if he knows about the hurricane. Today there are files and papers everywhere. It looks like he's emptied every last shelf onto the desks all over the room. I'm about to say hi until I realize he's on his classroom phone.

"Randy, I hear what you're saying and I'm telling

you the deed is not in the house." Dad shuffles through a file with his back to me. Even though I know it's not polite to eavesdrop, I can't help myself. I step just outside the doorway, press myself against the wall, and listen.

All I hear is Dad's side of the conversation and it goes like this:

"Of course we looked there. Anne and I looked everywhere. I even just ripped my classroom apart."

"I'm beginning to wonder myself if it ever existed."

"Are you kidding me? It's not an option. We have to find it and put an end to Throop's ridiculous claim."

"What do you mean, 'What if it's not ridiculous'? You honestly believe our father wanted to leave Throop the house? This is my life, Randy, my kids' lives we're talking about. You want us to surrender it all?"

"All right, you've made it abundantly clear how you feel. We don't need your help then. I'm done with this conversation."

Dad slams the phone onto the wall and I slip down the hallway before he can see me. It's pretty obvious what they were talking about. Uncle Randy still wants to give our home to Throop. I'm beginning to think Uncle Randy is the real traitor here, not Throop. I don't even know if I should trust Peter now.

I race home with my thoughts in a jumbled mess. When I walk in, Mom's wrapping up a call with her editor for her new project, and Jolene is at the table eating peanut butter crackers. Mom raises her eyebrows at me. I know what that means. I left my sister behind to walk home alone. But I have to wait until she's done on the phone to defend myself.

"I didn't leave school without her," I say. "Not on purpose. I went to talk to Dad, and Jolene must have thought I left."

"How was I sposed to know?" Jolene says. "You weren't by the bike rack."

"Please don't talk with your mouth full, Jolene," Mom says. "Savannah, you should have gotten your sister first and then gone to Dad's classroom. You knew Frankie was staying late today." She checks her watch. "And where is Dad? It's nearly four thirty."

"Um, I left before he did. He still had some things to finish up. Mom, Peter said there's a hurricane coming."

Mom takes a deep breath. "Yep, there is. We're making plans with your cousins to go up to Hatteras and Avon in the morning for supplies. It'll all be okay. You know the drill."

"We're going with Uncle Randy and Aunt Della?" I can't hide the surprise in my voice.

"Yes, we always go together and use Uncle Randy's truck. Why?"

I have no idea what to say to her except I think this time might be different. Just then Frankie walks in and I pull her into the living room. "I have to tell you something important."

Frankie sighs. "What is so important that I can't even set down my bookbag?"

"I got another message."

"A message from whom?"

"Blackbeard!"

"You used the Star Board by yourself? Why didn't you tell me?"

"I didn't really think anything would happen but I got a message: 'the brothers lose.' I asked Peter about it because I thought it might mean him and his brothers."

Frankie looks hurt.

I take her hand. "I'm sorry! You just seemed angry that night and I didn't want to make it worse. What do you think it means?"

Frankie doesn't look directly in my eyes. "I have no idea, Savvy. But I have a test to study for." She heads up the stairs to her room.

I don't know how, but somehow I've got to get my sister back.

In Search of Loot

The next morning, we all take a day off and our entire family—Peter's too, much to my surprise—takes a trip up the beach to Hatteras. The Outer Banks is a long strip of land with little towns all along it. Most of the towns are full of vacation homes, but Hatteras and Avon have a lot of year-round people. They have bigger food markets and hardware stores, so when a storm is coming, if we don't have to evacuate, everyone goes there for supplies.

I watch my dad and Uncle Randy closely and nothing seems terribly wrong despite the unfriendly conversation they had yesterday. It makes me wonder if I misheard it, or maybe they made up since. I really don't get grown-ups. But sometimes when Frankie and I get into a fight, it's like nothing happened the next day.

"I would have taken my own boat if it was running

better," Uncle Randy says as we sit in our cars on the ferry. He and Dad talk through the windows. "This is a madhouse."

"You know it probably won't even come near us. It'll probably turn at the very last minute like they always do," Aunt Della says over Randy's shoulder. "All this preparation for nothing every time really wears me down."

"Price you pay for being a fisherman's wife," Randy says, grinning. "Although, if I don't get the money to fix that boat, you may have to get used to being an unemployed man's wife!"

"Oh stop," Aunt Della says. "Everything will be fine."

"I remind myself every time how the rest of the year is pretty much perfect," Dad says. "It's only once in a while that we have to worry about these storms and we always get through."

No one says anything else.

The ferry heaves as it takes us across the inlet, almost an hour trip. Jolene falls asleep, and Frankie eventually gets out of the car and stares out over the railing at the choppy waves.

I slump in my seat and just wait.

Once the ferry docks, we drive off and up Highway 12 to Hatteras. Dad has a hard time finding a parking spot at the market. Eventually he parks near the back of the lot. He and Uncle Randy head off to get extra lumber, and Aunt Della, Will, and Peter head off for batteries and candles while we head to the market for everyone's food.

"We have to walk so far," Jolene whines. "I hate when we shop here."

"You can jump in the cart," Frankie says. "If we can find one."

Mom takes a cart from someone who just finished unloading, tears off two sections of her list, and hands one to me and Frankie. "Grab a basket if there are any left." But there aren't, so we have to gather as much as we can in our arms.

I head down the aisles to find one loaf of bread, six cans of tuna, and peanut butter for my first trip. The aisles are full of people, most of them pretty calm, but moving fast and weaving around one another to get what they want.

"Excuse me, ma'am," I say every time I bump into someone. "Sorry, sir." I'm able to find everything I need and then I have to figure out where Mom went. With my arms full, I walk past every aisle, peering down until I see Mom or Frankie, but I can't find either one. My arms get tired. I begin to think I should set everything down by the checkout when I look down aisle fourteen and see a familiar figure.

Dunmore Throop.

I gasp and it's like my hands forget how to work. All six cans of tuna drop to the floor, rolling in six directions. Under people's carts, between feet, and one slowly rolls all the way down the aisle right toward Throop. He looks up when it hits his shoe.

I can't stop staring at him, glaring at him, wishing I could melt him into the floor or something. He simply smiles at me, bends down to pick up the can, and starts to walk it over to me.

I quickly run back up the aisles, trying to find any of my family. Finally, there's Frankie in the cereal aisle with three boxes. I run up to her and grab her arms, almost knocking the cereal to the floor.

"What the heck, Savvy!" She pulls away. "Stop it!"

"You . . . you don't understand." I'm out of breath. "I saw him."

"Saw who?"

"He's here. He didn't leave!"

"Who?" Frankie looks confused and then worried. "You don't mean Throop?"

"Yes. Coffee and tea." I point. "He was just down there!"

Frankie sets her boxes down and runs with me, but of course he's nowhere to be seen. We look everywhere until we run into Mom and Jolene.

"Why are your arms empty? You got nothing from the list?" Mom asks. "What have you been doing all this time, girls? I want to get out of here—"

"Savvy saw Throop," Frankie blurts out.

Color leaves Mom's face, and then her eyes get fiery,

one eyebrow standing up as it always does when she's mad. "You're positive?"

I nod but Mom's eyebrow makes me nervous. "I think I'm positive?"

"You can't *think* you're positive," she says. "You either are or aren't."

"He looked like Throop. Tall, skinny . . ."

"Green hat?" Jolene asks.

I shake my head. "No." I start to doubt myself. Maybe it was just another tall, skinny man with dark hair. But he smiled at me like he knew who I was. Like he knew all my secrets.

"All right, let's just focus on getting our food, girls, so we can find your dad and cousins and go home," Mom says. She scans the market like an FBI agent as we walk through.

"If he was here and saw you, he probably took off," Frankie says. "He's smart enough to know not to come anywhere near us."

I'm not as sure as Frankie. I don't think Throop is afraid of anything. Just like any pirate, he's not going to stop until he wins. I know because I'm the same way.

After we find nearly everything on Mom's list, we check out and meet back up with Dad and Uncle Randy and Aunt Della, plus Peter and Will.

The second we're done, Jolene announces, "Savvy saw Throop," which sends the whole family into chaos.

My aunt and uncle and Peter ask me a hundred questions all at once.

I explain that it may not have actually been Throop and that he didn't do anything except pick up a tuna can.

Uncle Randy's face is as red as a stop sign. "Savannah, you need to get your story straight. Don't let your imagination run off with itself."

"I'm not!"

"We all know you have a bit of a history of embellishing things," he says. "People end up in trouble doing that."

"Randy," my dad interrupts, "Savvy wouldn't make up something so important. Either she saw Throop or someone who looked a lot like him. There's no need to blow this out of proportion."

Uncle Randy shakes his head and gets into his truck. I climb into the back seat of our van, near tears.

"Don't worry about him," Frankie whispers.

Jolene pats my hand. "Yeah, he's just grumpy." I don't say anything on the drive back to the ferry. I know it was Throop. The way he smirked at me—he recognized me for sure.

Once we're back on the ferry, I can't help but peek in as many cars as I can, just to make sure he's not following us home.

Batten Down the Hatches!

The wind starts picking up on Friday morning before the lighthouse cleanup weekend, creating tiny whirlwinds of sand and leaves. Since school is closed, lots of kids run around the village and Silver Lake Harbor watching the trees bend and the waves surge toward the docks. Some splash in puddles—Frankie and I ride our skateboards through them—but when the rain really gets rough, like needles on our skin, it forces us all inside. The hurricane isn't going to hit us directly, as Aunt Della predicted, but it's still a big storm and they can cause a lot of damage.

My parents already boarded some windows of the house with hurricane shutters and taped the glass of others the day before. They tied down anything outside, like the porch furniture and Jolene's swing set, so nothing would blow away. Everything seems to be holding up just fine. And so far even the power is still on.

Mom and Ms. Carolina Davis have started to become friends, so Mom takes candles and water next door and then sets out a ton of candles for us when she comes back. Dad keeps trying to fix the generator just in case we need it. We can hear it cough and sputter out in the garage and Dad says a few words I'd get in trouble for. The rain on the metal roof is loud but soothing as my sisters and I sit down with the clipper ship model I got for my birthday. It's thousands of pieces in little bags. Jolene takes one look and hops off her chair to go watch a cartoon. Frankie disappears upstairs shortly after.

I keep sorting through it, organizing the pieces as best as I can. A few years ago we had a much bigger hurricane and Grandpa and I did a whole thousand-piece puzzle of a sailing ship at the dining room table while the wind blew and rain battered the house. We almost evacuated for that one, but Grandpa insisted we'd be fine if we stayed. The Queen Mary, he said, could stand up to whatever weather came her way. Mom did not believe him, but Dad and Uncle Randy convinced her that we'd all be fine. After that storm, we'd only lost a small corner of the metal roof, but many neighbors had to do major repairs.

"I told you," Grandpa said. "This old house has seen it all."

Now my dad comes in from outside, soaking wet and frustrated.

"No luck?" Mom asks.

"None. Hopefully, if we lose power, it won't last terribly long."

"You mean *when*." Mom has never quite gotten used to the storms. She has a weather channel on in the kitchen and hasn't turned it off for hours.

Dad chuckles. "Don't worry, Anne." He wraps his arms around her. "It's not a bad one, I promise."

"Dad?"

"Yes, Savvy?"

"Remember Grandpa's metal detector?" After big storms, Grandpa would always go to the beaches with a special metal detector designed to find even the tiniest speck of gold.

"Do we still have that?"

"Yes, honey. I think it's in one of the upstairs hall closets."

"Can I go get it?"

Mom interjects. "You're not going outside right now, Savannah."

"I know, Mom, but after the storm, like Grandpa used to."

Dad nods. "Go ahead, sweetheart. Just be careful and put everything back where you find it."

"I wanna come!" Jolene, who was clearly listening, comes running in from the living room, and we run upstairs to check the closets. We must be pretty loud shifting things around, because Frankie comes out of her room in a huff.

"What exactly are you two doing?"

"Looking for Grandpa's metal detector," Jolene says.

"Why?"

"To see how it works," I say. "I'm going to take it out after the storm and search the yard." I drag out a few boxes into the hall to get to the detector.

"The yard? Why?"

"Why not?" The handle is sticking up in the corner of the closet but I can't quite reach it.

One of the boxes says PHOTOS on top and Frankie opens it while I struggle with pulling the metal detector out of the back corner. "I could use a little help here," I say. Frankie puts down a photo album and helps me and then goes back to the photos. The rain suddenly picks up outside, sounding like a train rushing toward us as it hits our roof.

"Check this out." Frankie shouts so we can hear her over the rain. "Grandpa and Grandma are so young."

Jolene and I sit on either side of her against the wall as she turns pages.

"Is that Dad and Uncle Randy?" I point to a photo with two young boys on a small white sailboat. One has a huge grin on his face and a gigantic fish in his arms as he looks directly into the camera. And the other is off to the side reading a book.

"What book is Daddy reading?" Jolene asks.

Frankie squints at the page. "Looks like *Treasure Island*."

"What?" I say. "No way. Dad said he was never into that stuff. Let me see."

Sure enough, this little version of my father is reading a book about pirates. And one that includes Blackbeard, no less.

"We saw that movie, right?" Jolene asks.

I nod my head. The one with the Muppets anyway.

"Grandpa gave me a copy but I never read it. It's really long," Frankie says. "And old. But the cover is pretty."

"Look, here's one with Grandpa, Grandma, and both Dad and Uncle Randy at some museum." I point to one of the faded pictures. Grandpa has a brass telescope in his hands and looks very proud.

Frankie turns through a few pages and later in the album, there's a photo that makes us all gasp. Grandpa and Dunmore Throop standing on a dock together. We know it's him because he's wearing that same green cap with the yellow anchor on it. And there's more. Grandpa and Throop on a beach. At some kind of award ceremony. The two of them on a huge boat called the *Brigantine*.

"That's Throop's boat," I whisper.

"How do you know?"

"Remember, he mentioned it a while ago? He made fun of me for thinking boats were all named after women. And he said that's the boat we met him on when we were little, before Jolene was born."

"Oh yeah." She flips through more pages.

In every photo with the young Throop, Grandpa seems so happy. There are more photos of Grandpa with Throop than Dad and Uncle Randy.

In one, Throop is wearing the celestial ring.

My skin grows hot. What if Grandpa stole it like he might have stolen Throop's sketchbook, and *that's* what Throop has been after? I roll the ring around between my fingers and then tuck it back under my shirt.

Outside there's a loud *bang*.

The wind knocked one of the hurricane shutters against the house. It must not have been fastened right. Jolene covers her ears. The banging gets louder and louder until suddenly it stops, like maybe the wind ripped it right off the hinges. And then all the power to the house goes out, leaving us in complete darkness.

We all scream.

The True Sea Dog

After Mom rescues us with candles, we all sit around the table looking at the photo album together. Rain and wind continue to pound the roof and windows, but it's cozy in the kitchen with the flickering candlelight. Even in the shadows I can see Dad has a strange look on his face, but Mom seems so happy to see the albums.

"Oh, Jack, you were so cute," she says. "Look at all those freckles."

"And look at Uncle Randy's chubby cheeks." Jolene giggles.

Dad snorts.

"Dad, why are there so many pictures of Throop in here?" I ask.

Dad leans back in his chair. "Well, he was Grandpa's business partner; you already know that."

"Yeah, but he's in the family photo album so much,"

Frankie says. "They seem like they were more like best friends than coworkers."

Dad nods. "Yes, they do, don't they?" He pushes away from the table. "I'm going to give that generator one last attempt. I just remembered something I haven't tried yet."

Mom hands him a flashlight so he can see as he goes down the hall. She sighs and turns the page in the album. Tapping a photo of Dad's whole family on a sand dune with kites, she says, "This one at Kitty Hawk is one of my favorites. I always thought your dad was so lucky to grow up here. All these wonderful little towns up the coast, so much history. And now you girls get to have it all, too."

"Dad doesn't seem like he thought it was all that great," Frankie says.

"Oh, he does." Mom turns another page and quiets her voice. "He's sore about Dunmore. He always felt Grandpa enjoyed spending time with Dunmore better than with your dad."

"Is that true?" I ask.

"They had a lot in common. They became very close friends and then worked together. I don't think it was a matter of liking him more than his sons, they just enjoyed each other's company."

"And Dad never really liked sailing or fishing," I say. "Definitely not treasure hunting."

"No, he's an anomaly around here," Mom says,

smiling. "But that's why I fell in love with him. He loves the poetry of the ocean if not the ocean itself."

There's a clanking outside and then Dad curses. It doesn't sound much like poetry.

Mom goes out to see if he needs help.

I pull a photo out of the album. It's the one of Grandpa and Throop at the award ceremony. It looks like it's an award for a sailboat race. On the back, in black ink, it says, "True Sea Dogs." Maybe Throop was like the son Grandpa always wanted. He sailed *and* he treasure hunted. Randy only wanted to fish and Dad only wanted to read about boats and treasure and pirates, not actually become one.

And then somewhere along the line, Throop turned on Grandpa. Or maybe Grandpa turned on Throop.

"I wonder what happened." I slide the photo back into the plastic sleeve. "It must have been bad to make Throop come after our house now."

"Sometimes friends aren't as good friends as you think," Frankie mumbles.

"What happened at school that day, Frankie?"

"I thought I could trust someone and it turns out I can't."

"Ryan?"

"No, but I'm not really talking to him anymore either." Frankie gets up and pours us all sweet tea. The wind howls outside. "Don't be mad, but I told Ashley and Dawn a little bit about the hunt."

Jolene gasps. "It's supposed to be a Dare family secret!"

"I know, but I thought we could use some help. Their families have been here as long as Grandpa's. I thought they might know something or know whom to ask."

I take a sip of my tea, cold and sweet, and crunch on an ice cube. I'm upset, but it means I can tell Kate. Grandpa used to say my sisters and I were strong because we were a cord of three. If a cord of three is strong, just think how much more if there were six of us. Or nine! "What did they say?"

Frankie shakes her head. "Let's just say they did not believe me. The more I tried to explain, the less they believed me. And then they started talking to everyone else, spreading rumors about our family."

"What's new," I say. Lots of people used to talk about Grandpa. Everyone liked him well enough, but no one took him seriously.

"I'm never talking to anyone ever again." Jolene slams her glass onto the table.

"Honestly, that won't really solve anything, Jolene," Frankie says. "I don't want to fight with my friends, but I have to be able to trust them." She runs a finger over the photo of Grandpa and Throop. "I just want this all to be over already so we can either prove or disprove it all and move on with our lives."

"We'll prove it," I say.

"Yeah." Frankie closes the album.

Suddenly there's a loud whirring sound like an engine starting up, and all the lights come back on. Dad got the generator going.

"Yeah is right," I say to Frankie. "As soon as this storm blows over, it's back to work."

"Aye-aye, Captain." Jolene salutes me. "Can we get a snack now?"

After the Storm

The next morning, the hurricane has blown by completely and the sun peeks through my curtains. Outside my window the sound of the generator rumbling and chain saws and voices pulls me to my feet. Mom and Dad, Ms. Davis, and a few other neighbors stand around a huge tree that came down between our properties, only inches from my bedroom window. How did I sleep through that, I wonder! I see tons of branches all over. Guess there won't be any metal detecting today. I also really wanted to talk to Kate about everything, but now I probably won't get the chance. I climb back into my bed and pretend to sleep. Mostly I'm still thinking about all the photos we saw last night and whatever happened between Grandpa and Throop.

"Savvy!" Mom bangs on my door a few minutes later. "Come on, kiddo. Time to get up. There's a ton to do."

I groan and pull the covers back over my head. "What do I have to do?"

"You and Frankie are in charge of stacking branches out by the road after we cut them. There's a blueberry muffin on the counter for you." Mom's footsteps fade away. A blueberry muffin sounds good, at least.

Once I dress and eat, I join everyone outside. It's cool and fresh, like the storm blew the last breath of summer out of the air overnight. The whole neighborhood seems to be out in the streets. Adults chatter about how bad it could have been and how we were lucky once again to lose only some trees and shingles.

After a few hours of dragging branches to the edge of the road, Mom gives me and Frankie money to go pick up four dozen clams and a bag of potatoes. "Dad's going to do them on the grill. We'll treat Ms. Davis too since none of us might have power for a few days," she says.

The seafood market is packed. We make our way to the counter, buy the clams, butter, and garlic, and Stan rings us up. "Have a good bake, girls!" he calls as we leave.

As we skate home after going to the co-op, Frankie has her backpack full of food and I carry the bag of potatoes. We pass a few kids from school and turn a corner and run right into Frankie's friends, Ashley and Dawn, on their bikes. They give us odd looks and I silently hope that they'll pass us by. But no such luck.

"So where are the Dare sisters off to today," Dawn says, braking her bike. "Robbing graves?"

She and Ashley crack up. They've been friends with Frankie since kindergarten. I'm surprised they're being so mean. Frankie looks like she's ready to explode but she skates right up to Dawn's bike. "Someday you'll regret this conversation," she says. And then she turns, pushes off, and skates away toward home.

"You heard her," I say, and follow my sister. I really hope Kate isn't going to be swayed by whatever rumors those two are spreading around. I have to talk to her as soon as I can, but probably won't get the chance until school opens back up on Monday.

Later that afternoon, once the adults have chainsawed through most of the fallen tree, Dad fires up the grill and puts foil-wrapped potatoes on. Mom chops onions and garlic, melts the butter, and puts it all together in a large bowl. Frankie and I set the table, and Jolene helps Mom rinse the clams. Everyone is strangely quiet as we work until Ms. Carolina Davis comes over for the first time ever.

"I don't know why we didn't do this sooner, Carolina," Mom says when we all sit down to eat.

"I reckon we never saw the need," Ms. Davis says. "I've always had my cats, and your family is always busy with three beautiful little girls to take care of. Life happens. No worries!"

"You and my father were good friends," my dad says, surprising me. I didn't know my parents knew this. Why had no one ever told me? "We should have had you over much sooner."

Ms. Davis lifts her sunglasses onto the top of her head, and I try very hard not to stare. There's nothing unusual about her face, but I guess that's why I'm surprised. Just bright blue eyes and a smile that seems even kinder now. "Oh, dear, dear Jack," she says. "Please don't worry yourself over an old woman like me. I didn't even have it in my weary heart to come to the memorial service; I was just too sad. That's on me, not you." She pats my dad's hand. Her eyes are watery. She puts the sunglasses back on and gets back to her clams.

"Ma'am," Jolene says, "may I ask you a question?"

Ms. Davis looks up at Jolene. "Why of course you can, angel."

"Why do you wear sunglasses at night?"

Mom nearly chokes on her food. But Ms. Davis just chuckles and pretends to look up at the sky. "Because the stars are so bright, don't you see?" It feels like exactly the kind of thing Grandpa would say. I decide she's a pretty cool neighbor.

After we're all done cleaning up, I walk Ms. Davis back to her porch, even though she insists she's fine.

"Ms. Davis, may I ask you something too?"

"Not about my glasses?"

I laugh. "No, ma'am. A serious question. When you and my grandpa were friends, I mean when you talked and played games and stuff, did he ever talk to you about a man named Dunmore Throop?"

Ms. Davis purses her lips together in thought. "Hmm, the name definitely sounds familiar. Was he the boat captain?"

"Maybe," I say. "Anything at all you can remember about him would be helpful."

"Cornelius used to talk about some young boat captain he was in a race with. I don't know where or what they were racing. Cornelius was too old to sail boats anymore, but he was angry that this young man was going to beat him."

I nod. "That has to be him."

"Can't say I remember much else. Why is it important to you?"

"Oh, no reason. His name just came up. We have a few pictures of the two of them together." I turn to go. "Night, ma'am."

"Good night, Savannah," Ms. Davis says.

Before I reach my porch, however, she calls out to me. "Oh, one thing just popped into my head that might be interesting to you!"

"Yes?"

"There was one night, years ago, when I was coming over to play Scrabble, and a young man was leaving. Your grandfather and he seemed to be in a heated conversation and I only remember because I had never seen Cornelius so angry before."

Had to have been Throop, I think. "Why was he angry?"

"I'm not sure, because when I asked Cornelius, he only mumbled something about how he couldn't trust anyone anymore, not even his own son." Ms. Davis shook her head, and my stomach seemed to drop out. "He wouldn't tell me anything else, and his mood brightened, so I didn't bother him about it. Figured it was some kind of family drama, like every family has."

"Yeah," I say, swallowing a lump in my throat. "Probably."

Was Throop trying to turn Grandpa against Dad or Uncle Randy? Certainly, Grandpa trusted Dad, considering we all moved in eventually. So, Uncle Randy?

I say good night again and go back to my house, my head swirling with more unanswered questions.

Carrying Out Orders

Since the storm didn't end up being too bad, the lighthouse cleanup day is postponed only to Sunday. That morning, as my sisters and I walk to it, Peter meets us down the road. "I've wanted to do this my whole life!" He rubs his hands together. "What's in the bag?"

It's hard for me not to ask him right away if he has any idea why his dad might have been fighting with Grandpa years ago. But it was so long ago, Peter probably has no idea. Besides, now isn't the time. "All our supplies. Flashlight, notebook and pencil, magnifying glass, and a towel," I say.

"Why a towel?"

"In case there are any artifacts in there, like the key. I want to wrap them up so they're safe in my bag."

"Wow," Peter says. "You think of everything."

"You're going to end up in tro-uble," Frankie says in a singsong voice.

"We have to at least try-y," I singsong back, adjusting my backpack to steady myself on the skateboard. We roll slowly so Peter can keep up. I'm going to have to find that boy a skateboard.

Frankie won't look at me. "If you get caught by a ranger, I'm pretending I don't even know who you are."

"So much for our pirate's oath!"

"Savvy, you know I will always be part of this, but I just don't believe Grandpa would set up anything in the lighthouse. Not only would the chances of your getting up there be slim, it's too dangerous."

"*It's too dangerous,*" I quietly mock. Frankie sounds more and more like a parent all the time. "It's a pirate treasure hunt! Of course it's dangerous!"

"We're like *Indiana Jones*!" Jolene says.

Frankie groans. "That's a movie, Jolene, not real life."

"Grandpa was a real-life treasure hunter, Frankie," I say.

Frankie skids to a stop right in front of me. "A treasure hunter who never found any real treasure."

"Doesn't mean he was wrong," Peter says. "I mean, he found a lot of really cool stuff."

I slip around Frankie and keep skating. "Thank you, Peter."

When we get to the lighthouse, people are all over

the place. Most are cleaning up leftover branches from the hurricane, but they seem close to finishing. The lighthouse door is open, but too many people are around to just go inside. We have to find the right moment. Mr. Baranski sees us and waves, so we head over to where he and a few kids from school are planting flowers.

"Glad to see you here, Dare family!" Mr. Baranski says. "Why, Jolene, I do love that eye patch!"

"Thank you, sir." Jolene salutes him. "Whatcha planting?"

"Well, we have a couple of native grasses and this flower here is called sweet pepper. They help feed the birds and bees and keep the sand from eroding." He hands Jolene a small shovel and offers one to me. "Would y'all like to help?"

Jolene takes the shovel, but digging in the sand reminds me of the night Frankie and I found the key. My arms ache just thinking about it. "I'm going to take a look around and see what other chores are happening," I say. Peter follows me, and Frankie stays with Jo. She gives me a quick warning look before I'm too far away and I give her a look back like, *I know what I'm doing*.

"So how do you want to sneak in?" Peter whispers as we get closer to the lighthouse.

"Let's see if anyone is even in there, first of all," I say. "Then we can make a plan." When we reach the door, I lean in. "Hello?"

"Hello!" a kind and cheery voice says back. A park

ranger in a green uniform with a name badge that says RODGERS steps into the light. "You kids want to take a look inside?"

"We can?" Peter asks, hopeful.

"Sure thing." Officer Rodgers steps aside. "Just stay off the stairs."

It takes a minute for our eyes to adjust to the dim light. It's a small space, most of it taken up by a giant metal spiral staircase right in the middle, which has a rope across the front. I take out my flashlight and shine it up. It looks like the steps disappear somewhere in the dark. A stairway to nowhere.

Peter tilts his head way back. "Whoa."

I swallow hard. It didn't seem that tall from the outside. "How many steps is that?" I ask Officer Rodgers.

"Only eighty-six," she says. "Pretty small for a lighthouse, and these aren't the original stairs. But she's one of the oldest working lighthouses in the country!"

Eighty-six steps doesn't sound so bad. I'm pretty sure I can climb that. Only, they look pretty old and rickety, as Mr. Baranski said in class. My stomach does unexpected flip-flops.

"Someone has to climb up there to check the light, right?" Peter asks.

"Yes, sir. Once or twice a year for maintenance. All the windows get washed. That sort of thing."

Peter and I look at each other. I know he's dying to go up too. We just have to get rid of this park ranger. We thank her on our way out and sit across the yard behind a big live oak where we can watch the door.

"She won't be in there forever," Peter says. "As soon as she's out, we make a run for it."

"What about a lookout?" I ask, glancing over at my sisters. "We always have a lookout."

"You don't think Frankie will do it?"

"You heard her; she's totally against this. And there's no way she'll let Jolene do it either."

"We'll be fine," Peter says. Just then Kate runs up and startles us both. She's carrying the board I gave her and I notice it has several more stickers.

"Hey! I've been looking for you two," she says. "Sav, you want to skate today? I don't have to be home till dark. Peter, you should come too!"

Peter looks at the ground. "Oh, thanks. But I actually don't know how."

"Savvy can teach you! She taught me." Before Peter has a chance to respond, she asks, "What are you two doing back here anyway?"

Peter and I look at each other and I know exactly what he's thinking. He's turning out to be a pretty good pirate after all. "Hey, Kate, wanna do us a favor?"

Bird's-Eye View

Peter explains the plan to Kate, telling her we just want to look out over the ocean.

Kate doesn't seem surprised or impressed. "It's not even really all that high."

Peter tilts his face to the sky. "Why does everybody say that!"

"I also want to see if I can find Theodosia, the ghost, for real," I tell her. "So what do you think? Will you be our lookout? And then we can all go to the park later."

Kate hugs her board and bounces. "I kinda want to see Theodosia too!"

"Then we're right back where we started!" Peter says. "This time you be lookout, then we'll switch if there's time. I'll go up twice!"

"What exactly would I have to do?"

"Just stand near the door and if a ranger comes by, whistle real loud."

"You'll never get back down in time," Kate says, looking at me.

"It's better than nothing," I say. I know we'll be in trouble if we get caught, but we have no choice if we want to search for clues. "And you don't have to stick around. I don't want you to get into trouble. Just whistle and run."

Kate shakes her head. "Okay. You two come up with the strangest ideas."

"It runs in the family," Peter says, making us both laugh. Then he says to Kate, "Your board looks really cool." I think it's pretty unusual for him to say something nice like that. But it makes Kate smile.

After about ten more minutes of our talking and waiting, the ranger finally comes out and heads toward the keeper's house.

"Now's our chance." I stand up and dust the sand off my legs.

"Now or never!" Peter says. And we start walking toward the lighthouse.

"Just act natural." We probably look like robots walking across the yard, the three of us side by side, trying not to seem suspicious. I glance over at my sisters really quick to see if Frankie sees us, but they're busy listening to Mr. Baranski and have their backs to us.

We reach the door and one by one walk right in and hide in the shadows.

"I'm going to be right here," Kate says, standing half in the doorway and facing the lighthouse keeper's house, "so I can see if anyone is coming. I'll whistle, like we planned."

"Perfect," Peter says. He unlatches the rope and steps onto the first metal stair. "Ready, Sav?"

"I'm ready." I follow Peter and begin counting as we go. "One, two, three . . ."

"What are you doing?" he asks.

"If I count them, I'll know when I'm almost to the top . . . twelve, thirteen . . ."

Our footsteps echo in the chamber of the lighthouse, so I try to walk quieter and slower but it still makes noise. The entire staircase vibrates a tiny bit with each movement. Gripping the railing, I silently talk to Grandpa as I also count. *If you went up here, then you surely know it's safe for us. I know you'd never lead me into real trouble, Grandpa. Twenty-two, twenty-three . . .*

"Oh cool!" Peter stops and leans over the railing. My stomach does a somersault. "Look down!" He points.

"That's okay. I'm good," I say, and keep counting my footsteps on the clanging metal. I've climbed trees and been on speedboats and dived through waves and zoomed down ramps on my board, but I never knew, until this very moment:

I, Savannah Mae Dare, am afraid of heights.

"Forty-two, forty-three . . . halfway there," I say more to myself than Peter. He's basically running up the spiral stairs now, which makes the whole thing rattle more. "Peter! Can you slow down?"

He stops and looks at me like it's the strangest thing I've ever said. "Sorry!"

"Sixty-nine, seventy, seventy-one . . ." I begin thinking, what if we really did run into Theodosia. Would she be friendly? Would she let us pass? Would she topple us back down the steps like dominoes?

Finally, finally, finally, I reach the eighty-sixth step. The ranger was right on the nose. There's a platform up top with very little room to move around the lens. The light is off right now, so we don't have to worry about blinding ourselves. Peter is already spying out the window and shouting out all the things he can see. "There's the school! And my house!"

I look around for a message, or an artifact, or hidden clue of any kind. Maybe a rock that slides out of the wall? But I run my hands along it, and every brick is solid. Maybe a crack along the window where Grandpa could have hidden a note? But everything is sealed tight.

"What if that ranger already found whatever Grandpa left?" I ask.

"Or maybe there's something on the outside?" Peter points out the window. There is a tiny ledge and railing around the outside.

"No. Way." I draw the line at climbing out there. I hate to admit it, but I think Frankie was right. Grandpa didn't leave anything up here for us, or if he did, someone else got to it already, and it wouldn't be on the outside on that teeny-tiny ledge. Grandpa would never do that. I grab Peter's arm. "What if Throop got here first?"

"How would he get in?"

"Maybe the last cleaning? Or, who knows, maybe he's friends with a ranger? Maybe he picked the lock."

"No, think about it, Savvy, he wouldn't have been chasing after you if he already had the clues."

"That's precisely why he might be after us. To get the rest of them!" Although looking around the platform now, I just can't imagine what Grandpa would have left here. There's no place to hide anything. I might have been wrong about the important window.

Just then there's a shrill whistle from way down at the bottom.

Kate.

Peter shouts, "*Go!*" But I glance at the spiral staircase. It looks like it disappears into an abyss. I can't move my feet.

Peter gently pushes past me and tries to coax me down the steps. "You can do it; come on!"

But I can't. I can't even move. I shake my head but can't speak.

"Savvy, we have to go. Here, let me help you." Peter takes me by the wrist and leads me down one stair at a time. We're about thirteen steps down when suddenly there is a loud bang below us. I cower.

Everything goes black.

Someone, or something, has shut us inside the lighthouse.

Kate Comes Aboard

A million possibilities run through my mind. Who locked us in? The ranger? Throop? Kate? The wind? Theodosia's ghost? Neither of us move at first because we can hardly see the stairs now, but once our eyes re-adjust, we continue our way down.

"It'll be fine, we'll be fine, it's all fine," Peter talks to himself as he goes.

"We'll just bang on the door," I say. "Someone will hear us."

"I hope you're right."

"Kate knows we're in here!"

"You told her to whistle and run," Peter says. "She might not realize we're trapped."

My heart beats so fast and I do not want to start crying, so I stop thinking about it. I grab Peter's shirt. "Just go," I say. "Just get us to the bottom."

Our feet *clang, clang, clang* as we stomp all the way down the metal steps. This time I don't mind all the noise and I push the thought of how high we are out of my brain. Peter leads the way and reaches the door first. He starts pounding on it. "Hey, can anybody hear me? We're in here!"

I join him and pound my fists as hard as I can. "Open the door! Hello? Anyone?"

Our voices echo through the lighthouse and for a long minute I'm afraid we've really done it this time. It's hard to breathe and it's so dark. Then suddenly the door swings open. Bright light blinds us at first and I hold an arm up so I can see better. The ranger stands there staring at us, clearly confused. Kate and Mr. Baranski, Frankie and Jolene are all behind her. Everyone looks a combination of worried and angry. My face burns. I'm sure I'm bright red.

"How in the world did you two get stuck in there?" Officer Rodgers asks as she motions for us to get out. "Y'all are very lucky people are still around!"

"Sorry, ma'am," Peter says. I apologize too. The ranger seems frustrated but shakes her head and doesn't say anything else except for us to get our butts home. We duck out of the lighthouse so she can relock the door and face Frankie's very angry face next.

"I hope that was worth it, Savannah," she says through clenched teeth. I shake my head no. But she doesn't say, "I told you so," as I thought she would, so that's nice of her at least.

"Let's go home," she says instead.

Kate and Peter walk with us. "I tried to give you as much warning as I could," Kate says. "I saw the ranger coming, whistled up, and hid around back. I didn't know what else to do."

"It's fine," I tell her. "It was a little scary at first, but we're okay. You did everything right."

Jolene takes my hand. "Savvy, what was it like at the top?"

"Very small," I say. "Not a lot of room. And there's *nothing* up there except the big lens. I was wrong."

Jolene's shoulders slump.

"I think Theodosia only comes out at night," Kate says, trying to make me feel better. "So chances were pretty slim that you'd get to see her, Savvy."

I feel bad keeping secrets from her, and I can tell from the look on Peter's face it's nearly killing him to not tell her the truth. I look at Frankie and she shrugs, which I think is permission.

So, as we walk home, we finally tell Kate everything.

From Grandpa's stories when he was alive to the treasure map he left us, the key we found, and the rest of the clues, I tell her everything we know so far about Blackbeard's treasure and Dunmore Throop. I even tell her about the messages on the Star Board probably being from the real ghost of Blackbeard the pirate.

When I'm done, her eyes are wide and unblinking. She opens her mouth to say something and then shuts it.

"What are you thinking?" I ask. "You believe me, right?"

Kate looks at my sisters and Peter, who nods and says it's all true.

"I mean, if you all say it's true, how can I not believe you?" But Kate still seems a little unsure.

I take my backpack off, reach inside, and pull out a burlap-wrapped object.

"Savannah!" Frankie scolds. "What were you thinking, taking that from the house?"

"I knew it would be safe," I say, unwrapping the gold key, which is about the size of a fork. Everyone circles around.

Kate runs a finger across the little gems on it. "Wow," she whispers. "It is real. That's beautiful. What do you think it's for?"

"We've had so many ideas," I say. "Maybe a chest on the *Queen Anne's Revenge*. We're not sure. I wondered if it was for something up in the lighthouse, which is one of the reasons we went up. A cabinet or a safe or something! But I guess I should have known it wouldn't be that easy." After everyone gets a good look, I wrap it back up and hide it in the bottom of my bag.

"What's your next step?" Kate asks.

"Figuring out what the code word 'window' means," Peter says. "Because this wasn't it."

Kate keeps asking questions, which we all answer

as best as we can. When we reach the cemetery, Jolene pulls on my shirt.

I need time to think and relook at the map and all the things we have from Grandpa so far. But she's persistent and yanks hard until I look at her. "Jolene, what?!"

She points to the tombstones, and in the far corner there's a man crouched near one of the old gravesites. He holds a piece of paper against the stone and rubs some kind of dark chalk or paint on the paper. As we get a little closer, I know exactly who it is.

I pull my little sister into the shadows of the closest house. "No way," I whisper.

"It's him," Frankie says, and stops in her tracks. "It's Throop." The rest follow us into the shadows and we stand and watch him.

"What's he doing?" Kate asks.

Frankie whispers back, "I think he's doing a gravestone rubbing. It's when you rub charcoal on the paper and it picks up the words from the tombstone."

"Why would he want to do that?" Peter asks. "He could just take a picture."

"Maybe he doesn't have a camera with him," Jolene says.

"It's kind of an old-fashioned thing," Frankie says. "Grandpa had a couple of rubbings in all his stuff, Savvy; you probably saw them."

Kate shivers. "Creepy."

I don't remember seeing any gravestone rubbings in Grandpa's things, but it definitely sounds like something he would have done. "We have to wait until he's done so we can go see what's on that tombstone," I say.

Someone's stomach growls, which makes Jolene cover her mouth and giggle, even though it was probably hers.

"Shhh!" I pull her down to the ground and we all crouch low and wait. Kate and Peter sit next to each other on her skateboard. A car goes by. A family of four on bikes. A couple walks by holding hands—they're the only ones who turn and actually look at us. We all smile and they keep walking.

After a few more minutes, Throop finally packs up his things. He moves quickly, tosses the charcoal and other small items into his bag, and then rolls the paper into a cardboard tube. He looks around, seems to feel like the coast is clear, and then dashes off between the tombstones, hurtles himself over the low wall, and disappears into the woods.

"Let's go!" I say, and dart across the road, not taking my eyes off the tombstone Throop stood at. When I reach it, I see there are symbols following the arch of the stone; little suns, moons, and swirls and what looks like letters from a different language. For a gravestone, it's very pretty. When everyone catches up, I read the inscription out loud:

Here lies Benjamin Samuel Hort
He traveled the world, never to port
Oft hailed a handsome bloke
Only to die on Ocracoke
1820–1866

"Who's Benjamin Hort?" Kate asks.
I shrug. "No idea."
But I have the feeling I better find out.

Fire in the Hole!

The next day, we're putting our skateboards away after school when Ms. Carolina Davis comes out of her house with an armful of books. "Girls! I finally remembered!" She rushes over with the stack and places them in Frankie's arms. "I regret I never got through all these, but I wanted to make sure to return them to the rightful owners."

"It's really not a problem if you want to keep them a little longer," Frankie says.

Ms. Davis shakes her head. "No, no, no, these are honestly more your grandfather's tastes than mine. He wanted me to hang on to them for safekeeping, but I suppose he forgot about them. I prefer romance novels."

Jolene scrunches her nose. I give her a look to stay quiet. The books in Frankie's arms are mostly about ships and sailing, not exactly fun reading, but I can understand why Grandpa would love them. One of them is called *Celestial Navigation,* which sounds cool—it's about finding your way by using the sun and stars.

"Thank you, Ms. Davis," Frankie says, and carries the books inside. She dumps them onto the dining room table and we go into the kitchen for a snack. But when we walk into the room, both Mom and Dad are folding laundry. They've clearly been waiting for us and they don't look happy.

"What now?" I say when I see their faces.

Mom sets down the towel she's folding. "How about you tell us?"

Frankie and I look at each other. Jolene starts crying before we even know what we're in trouble for.

"Did you honestly think word wouldn't eventually get out about two kids in the lighthouse?" Dad says, and tosses me a pillowcase to fold. Frankie pulls out a few T-shirts to help.

"Oh. That," I say.

Mom's eyebrow arches. "Yes, that. Didn't we have a talk about letting us know if this little treasure hunt was going to take you somewhere you shouldn't be?"

"Yes, ma'am."

"And do you think it's right you roped your cousin into helping you? Which has infuriated your uncle all over again, I might add."

"No, ma'am."

"Then what were you thinking?"

I place the folded pillowcase on the pile, and Dad hands me another. "I was thinking if I asked permission, you and Dad would say no."

"Well, you were at least thinking right about that!"

"But I had to know if anything was at the top!"

"And was there?"

I shake my head and fold the second pillowcase in silence.

"The three of you are grounded," Dad says. "One week. Home immediately after school. Chores and homework and that's it."

"Dad!" Frankie says. "Savannah went up, not us!"

"And did you know about it and not tell anyone?"

"Ugh!" Frankie gives me a dirty look. "This is so unfair." She tosses the unfolded shirts back into the basket and stomps off to her room.

"Yeah!" Jolene follows Frankie. I don't know what she's angry about. She can't go anywhere without us anyway. I sit at the table and put my chin on my arms. This is my fault, but I had to do it. Even though I didn't find anything. Still, I hate disappointing everyone. Seems like I constantly do that.

"Sorry," I mumble. "I didn't mean to get my sisters into trouble."

Mom pushes over a pair of jeans. "Frankie got herself in trouble by deciding to keep it a secret."

"I guess."

"Look, Savvy, if we can't trust you with this, I'm going to take away the map and put an end to it. Your aunt and uncle are livid," Dad says.

I sit up straight. "Dad! No! I'll be more careful. I promise. I won't ask Peter to do anything dangerous again."

My parents don't look like they entirely believe me, but they nod and let me go to my room. "Please take those books and put them away up on one of the shelves in the living room before you go up."

"Okay." Once four of them are shelved, I decide to take the last one, *Celestial Navigation,* to my room, now that I'm a prisoner for a week and I like reading what Grandpa liked to read.

Upstairs, Frankie plays music really loud in her room behind the closed door. I almost knock to apologize but then decide to just let her cool down first. When I pass Jolene's room, she's curled up with a stuffed dog and our real dog, Py, so I don't bother her either. I quietly close the door to my own room and spread out on my bed with the book.

Unfortunately, Ms. Davis was right. It's really boring.

But some diagrams of constellations and pictures of old navigation tools are kind of cool. There are notes in the margins here and there—Grandpa's curly writing. Mostly I page through not really reading but thinking about how Grandpa one time turned the same pages and probably understood everything he read. He knew so much about the most random, interesting things and told us so many stories. But I can't help but think he had so many more that we'll never hear.

Flipping toward the back, I find a cool photo of an old sailing ship that reminds me of the one in the dream I had about Grandpa. But what really catches my attention is that in the description of it, the letter "r" is circled in black ink. Curious, I go back to the beginning of the book and flip through to look closer at the other descriptions of illustrations and diagrams. Almost all of them have a letter circled! I grab a notebook and pencil and carefully page through the entire book—all four hundred pages!—until I've written down every circled letter. Fortunately, there aren't too many, but they don't make any sense all together.

Olfomeolphaovembereltaikelphaikelphaomeoankeeie rraapalphandiaovemberangondiaovemberolf

There seem to be patterns, like "olf" and "ovember," but no real words. Maybe they mean "wolf" or "November," but it doesn't make any sense to me. Grandpa never makes it easy, but I'm sure he'd leave some kind of clue as to how to solve this, so I continue looking, reading the copyright page, the index, the author's note, everything.

I close it and read the spine: *Celestial Navigation* by B. S. Hort.

We just saw that name! Or close to it. Benjamin Samuel Hort. On the gravestone. I scramble off the bed, gathering the book and paper.

"Frankie, open up!" I bang my fist on her door. She turns the music up louder. So I run over to Jolene's room and shake her awake. She rolls over but I make her focus on me. "I need you to knock on Frankie's door."

Jolene yawns. "Why?"

"It's important. I'll explain once we get Frankie."

Jolene hops out of her bed, pads over to Frankie's room, and knocks on the door. "Frankie? Are you in there?"

We hear Frankie through the door. "I know Savannah sent you! Go away!"

I lean against my sister's door. "Frankie, this is really important! I found . . ."

Mom shouts up, "Savannah Mae! Stop all the banging and shouting!"

I yell down the hall. "It's *really important* and Frankie won't open her door!"

Then suddenly she does. And I'm flat on my back looking up into her very red and angry face. "Hi," I say.

"Get up and get in here."

I get up off the floor, and Jolene comes in. All three of us sit on Frankie's bed. "What now?" she asks.

After I'm done explaining, Frankie has a look on her face I don't understand. "What?" I say. "It's another clue."

"A clue that was over at Ms. Davis's house this whole time?"

"I guess."

"That doesn't make sense."

Jolene flops back on Frankie's bed. "None of it ever makes sense," she whines.

"I guess it's strange. But she said something about safekeeping. Or maybe he forgot he lent the book to her. Maybe he thought he'd get it back before . . . you know . . . he died."

"Or maybe it has nothing to do with us or the treasure hunt," Frankie says. "Maybe it's something else entirely."

I shake my head. "The only way to be sure is to figure it out." I point to the author's name on the book. "Besides. Look at this."

Jolene leans up and looks too. "Whoa. Shiver me timbers," she says. "Short!" She runs her finger across the whole name and sounds it out. "If you ignore the B, look what you get. S. Hort. Sh . . . ort! It's the answer to Grandpa's third riddle."

We're all quiet for a minute. Short was really B. S. Hort? But why?

"I'm totally lost," I say. "It's like we skipped a clue but somehow ended up with the answer anyway."

Frankie nods. "I also think we need to tell Mom and Dad what we saw Throop doing at the cemetery before they figure that one out and we get into more trouble."

I fold up the strip of paper with the code and shove it into my pocket. "Yeah, I guess you're right." I hate admitting when Frankie is right.

Swimming in Circles

Telling Mom and Dad just makes them even more frustrated with us, so on top of being grounded for a week, now we're not allowed to go anywhere alone until the court case is done or we know Throop has given up and is gone.

"How are you going to know he's gone?" Frankie asks. "We all thought he left already!"

"I don't know," Dad says.

"Ugh!" Frankie sighs again. "I can't even believe how unfair this is. I thought being honest would help."

"I'm glad you were honest. It helps us know how serious Dunmore is about getting our house," Mom says. "What was he doing, exactly?"

"A grave rubbing," I tell her. "Who is Benjamin Samuel Hort?"

Both of my parents shake their heads. "No idea."

I drop the *Celestial Navigation* book onto the table. "Well, we think he's the author of this book." Frankie looks at me, probably wondering if I'm going to say anything about the circled message inside. I decide not to; I want to solve it first. Solving a code doesn't hurt anyone or put anyone in danger because I can do it in my room all by myself, so my parents can't get mad about that. Besides, even Frankie said it might be completely unrelated to our treasure hunt.

Dad flips through the pages, but not enough to notice the markings. "Interesting. I remember your grandpa studying this book, ages ago. Ms. Davis had it?"

"She said Grandpa lent her a bunch of books she never read."

He slides it over to Mom. "Can't blame her there."

Mom picks up the book and sticks it into her bag. "I'll take it to the library tomorrow and talk to Mr. Brown, see what we can dig up about Hort."

I start to protest but then let it go.

Once they're satisfied that we've told them all we know, we help make dinner and talk about other stuff for a while. School, Dad's work—which is more school—and Mom's new projects. Jolene talks about how much she loves her teacher, plus how I've been teaching her to skate by herself, and Frankie tells us about her research project for English.

I mostly listen. Or half listen. I'm too distracted by

the letters in my head and trying to figure out what the trick might be to interpret them.

Dad finally asks, "What's up, Savvy? You're too quiet tonight."

I shrug. "Just thinking."

"Want to elaborate?"

Not really, but I say, "Thinking about Grandpa's codes. The different puzzles he used to give me that spell out special messages."

"That's a nice memory," Mom says. "He certainly loved challenging you girls."

"Maybe too much," Frankie says, and laughs.

We start eating and I don't say anything for a while, but eventually I have to ask. "Mom, you know words . . ."

Mom laughs. "Yes, I do. Is there a vocabulary word you need help with?"

I pull the folded paper out of my pocket. "Sort of. Do you know what language this might be?" I slide it over to her.

She gives me a funny look. "These aren't really words, Savvy."

"Yeah." I take a big sip of water and look over at Frankie, who's focusing on her dinner instead of looking at me. "There are patterns, though. See?"

Mom and Dad both look at the paper. "This one is sort of like November," Mom says. "It's in there three times."

"And the 'olf' reminded me of 'wolf,' " I say.

Dad taps on the paper. "Or 'golf.' Where did you find this, Savvy?"

"Oh." I take a big gulp of water and look at Frankie, who shrugs. "It was in one of Grandpa's books." Only half a lie.

"Makes sense then. There are some letters missing, but this looks like part of the military alphabet," Dad says.

"What's that?" I ask.

Dad rips a piece of bread off the warm loaf in the center of the table and spreads butter on it. "Each word stands for a letter. It makes communication easier when talking over radios or telephone because letter sounds are easily mixed up. It was created for pilots originally, I believe. 'Alpha' is 'A,' 'Bravo' is 'B,' 'Charlie' is 'C,' and so on." He slides the paper back to me.

"Oh yes," Mom says, reading over my shoulder. "Look, here is 'lpha' four times, which must be 'Alpha,' which would really be an 'A.' "

Suddenly I can't sit still. "Do you know what all twenty-six are?"

Dad thinks for a moment. "Most of them, but there's probably a list in your grandpa's office somewhere. Maybe in his desk or in one of his notebooks. Why, are you planning to join the air force?" He grins at his own joke.

"No. But I'm going to figure out what this says and it might be fun to make up a puzzle with it!" I say, trying to sound cheery and innocent and like I have no secrets to hide whatsoever. Nope, not "Savvy" Savannah Mae.

I fold up the paper and put it back into my pocket and say nothing more about it as we finish eating and help clean up. Frankie and I have homework, so we sit at the table for that and eventually, after what feels like the longest night ever, I go up to my room to get ready for bed. But instead of putting on my pajamas, I go into Grandpa's office and search his desk. It used to be pretty messy, but after he died, Mom cleaned and organized everything in the drawers. There are a bunch of notebooks full of his curly writing and slips of paper he wrote on when he began forgetting things, small sketches of maps, some photos of me and my sisters. Finally, I find a worn, green, postcard-size chart of each letter and the word that stands for it in the military alphabet.

"Yes," I whisper to the ceiling. "Thank you, Grandpa." I run it back to my room and compare it with the letters I found. It's actually very simple to solve after all.

Golf Romeo Alpha November Delta Mike Alpha Mike Alpha Romeo Yankee Sierra Papa Alpha India November Tango India November Golf

Grandma Mary's Painting.

Grandma Mary's painting is the portrait she did of Grandpa when he was younger, which hangs in our dining room. Once everyone goes to bed, I know exactly what I have to do. And this time I'll do it alone so I don't get my sisters into trouble.

My alarm goes off at one in the morning. When it rings, I don't even remember where I am or why I'm waking up in the dark. I quickly turn it off and begin to wake up fully and remember my mission.

Sneaking downstairs is tricky. There're two or three very squeaky steps that I skip altogether and that makes me nearly slip on my socks on the way down, but I hold on to the rail just in time. At the bottom I pause and listen. The Queen Mary is silent except for Py softly snoring on the couch. I'm sure no one heard me, so I tiptoe into the dining room and walk up to Grandpa's handsome portrait.

It's a huge painting, probably taller than Jolene, and has a heavy wooden frame. I drag a chair over, stand up, and gently lift it from the wall. Carefully I place it on the dining room table and get a flashlight from the kitchen. I examine the entire painting, shining the light on every inch of Grandpa's face.

Py comes over and curls up at my feet. After a few minutes of finding nothing unusual, I carefully flip the painting over to look at the back, which is covered in a thin brown paper. It looks totally clean, no words, numbers, or anything except in the bottom left-hand corner, the paper is folded up just a tiny bit.

"Grandpa, I got the lighthouse wrong, so I sure hope

this is what you wanted me to do," I say as my finger gently lifts the paper from the frame, peeling it back like a bandage off skin, as carefully as I can. It's impossible to not rip it a little, and I figure I'll have to glue it back down after I'm done.

Between the canvas and the brown paper is a yellow envelope with little metal clasps. I hold my breath and cover my mouth so no sound can escape. Fortunately, Py's on my feet, otherwise I don't know how I'd keep from jumping up and down. The problem is that the only way to get that envelope out is to take off the rest of the paper backing.

"Hopefully Mom and Dad won't notice," I whisper to Py, and gently tear back the rest of the paper. The envelope is about the same size as the first one we got from Grandpa, the one he'd left in the care of Mrs. Taylor at the historical society a few weeks ago, which started this whole treasure hunt. But this one doesn't have any messages or names written on it. Just blank.

I throw the paper in the garbage and hang the portrait back up. Py follows me up to my room and we both climb onto the bed. I keep the lights off, hide under the covers, and hold a flashlight between my shoulder and neck as I open the envelope.

Inside is a whole new map. And this one isn't of Ocracoke. It's not like a regular map; there don't seem to be any towns or anything labeled at all. Only a lot of squiggly lines, numbers, and strange, random angles drawn over water and land. I don't recognize any of it and there's not a single word printed on it.

I reach back inside the envelope and find a really long strip of paper all folded up, which when unfolded has letters written down the entire length with random spaces between. This I recognize right away. It's called a scytale cipher. The strip of paper gets wrapped around something round and the letters line up so you can read it. I just have to figure out what Grandpa used to wrap the paper around, which might be tricky, because it has to be the same size. We made them together with paper towel tubes but I don't imagine Grandpa would do that for something so important.

Then again, he made this entire treasure hunt for us, with clues only we would know. Dunmore Throop would *never* suspect a paper towel tube as a decoding tool.

I jump out from under the covers, tiptoe back downstairs, and unravel an entire roll of paper towels. I think Mom just opened that roll up at dinner, so I'll just have to tell her I needed the tube for a school project. I try to fold the paper towels up as neatly as I can, but it's basically a ginormous pile in the middle of the table. Quietly as I can, I head back up the stairs.

And run right into my dad.

He looks confused. "Savvy, what are you doing up this time of night?"

"Um, I needed a drink of water?"

Dad looks at the cardboard tube in my hands. "Were you planning to drink out of that?"

"No. It's for a project I forgot about."

Dad just shakes his head. "It's too late to be working on schoolwork. You need to get back to bed."

"Okay." I start to walk down the hall but turn and go back to give him a quick hug.

"What was that for?" he asks.

"Just thought you might need it."

He smiles. "Night, Savvy."

Back under my covers, where Py still waits, I lay the flashlight on the bed and tape one end of the strip of paper to the top of the tube. Then I slowly wrap the strip of paper around the tube. Just as I thought, the letters all line up and I can read them vertically.

R		C		W
I		H		I
N	+	A	+	N
G		R		D
		T		O
				W

Ring, chart, window. The ring *has* to be the celestial ring Dad gave me, although I have no idea how Grandpa knew he'd give me the ring. And I assume this chart behind Grandpa's portrait is the important chart! I throw the covers off and nearly scream, I'm so excited. I jump down and open my door, ready to run into Frankie's room and wake her up. I can't believe our luck!

Until, all of a sudden, I realize there's one very big problem.

We're in the same exact boat as before—we still have no idea what the window is.

Hanging by a Thread

On the weekend, since we're almost at the end of our grounding, I ask Mom if it's okay for Peter and Kate to come over to our house for lunch. I'm so excited to show everyone the new map that it feels like my insides are buzzing.

"Long as you all stay right here, in the house or on the porch, yes," she says.

"Mom, did you find out anything about that book?"

"I finally stopped at the library briefly yesterday. The only thing Mr. Brown and I came up with was a few other books by the same author. Nothing groundbreaking. I actually put it back up on the shelf with the others if you'd like it back."

"Hmm, no. I'm good. But thanks for trying." I don't need the book as much as I need to know why it was at Ms. Davis's house. "I have another question."

"Hopefully I have an answer for this one," she says.

I pull the celestial ring out. "You know how Grandpa gave this to Dad and he gave it to me?"

"Yes."

"In the photos we were looking at the night of the hurricane, Throop was wearing it. Do you think Grandpa stole it?"

Mom tilts her head. "I doubt it. Grandpa wasn't a thief. Maybe there were two rings?"

"I didn't think of that." If there are two rings, and Throop already has one, maybe it was the envelope behind the portrait that he wanted.

When this all began, I wanted to keep it between my sisters and me but now, with so many clues going nowhere, the more brains working together the better. It's time to have a serious pirate meeting.

Kate arrives first and Jolene runs up to her and grabs her hand. "I'll show you around!"

"Jolene, Kate has been here before," I say.

"But it's been a long time and we've moved some things around," Jolene insists.

"It's okay," Kate calls out as she's yanked into the next room. "I like looking at all the stuff your grandpa found!"

Mom's in her office and lets us take charge of lunch. We decide to keep it simple: ham and cheese sandwiches. I get out the bread and cheese, and Frankie gets the mustard and mayo. "Savvy, what exactly do you have planned?" she asks me as she rips off a paper towel from the pile I made the other night. I think Mom is so used to me creating weird things she never even asked me where the cardboard tube went.

"You'll see." I raise my eyebrows like Mom. "I've made some very important discoveries."

Frankie looks skeptical, but she doesn't say anything else. Just then Peter bounds into the kitchen. "Hey! Where is everyone?"

"Kate is being dragged around by the One-Eyed Wonder currently," Frankie says. "But other than that, you're looking at it."

"Oh cool. Kate's here? Kate's really cool," he says, shifting his weight. His face suddenly turns a little pink.

"Peter Dare," I whisper. "Do you have a crush on Kate Roberts?"

"Shut up, Savannah," Peter says. "What's for lunch and what's the plan anyway?"

Frankie hands Peter a plate. "Savvy said she's made some discoveries."

"Sure did," I say, grinning at Peter. "But you'll have to tell the truth about Kate if you want to hear them."

"Savannah," Frankie starts to warn me, but then Jolene and Kate return to the kitchen and we all drop it.

"Let's take our sandwiches upstairs," I say. "And then I'll tell you everything."

We all make up our plates—ham and cheese, pickles

and chips—and go up to the attic, where I already have Grandpa's original Ocracoke map and the Star Board set out. The new envelope I found is tucked under the Star Board.

"So, clearly this Hort person is super important," Kate says. "And the guy in the graveyard the other day knows it."

"Yes," I say.

"Is Throop really dangerous?" Kate asks.

"I don't know," I say. "Part of me is a little afraid of him, but now that I've seen all the photos of him and Grandpa together, the other part wonders if there's a different side to Throop."

"It's definitely strange to think he was really good friends with Grandpa," Frankie says.

Peter swallows his last bite and dusts off his hands. "So what's the new discovery, Savvy?"

I smile and slide the envelope out from beneath the Star Board. "This was behind Grandpa's portrait downstairs."

"What do you mean?" Frankie asks. She opens it and unfolds the chart.

I explain to them all how I discovered the code in the book and it led me to Grandpa's portrait. I show them the cipher message too. "I never would have found this if Ms. Davis hadn't returned that book, which means there's probably a clue we didn't find that would have led us to it."

"So somehow Ms. Davis is part of this?" Kate asks as she pops open a bag of chips.

I shrug and slide my plate under the couch. "I think more likely Grandpa just didn't get the book back in time to set it up where he wanted. But we have it now. And as cool as these new hints are, we haven't really gotten anywhere. So I think it's time to ask Blackbeard again."

Kate stops chewing midbite. "Are you being serious?"

Jolene lifts up her eye patch to look at Kate better. "Savvy is always serious."

"I always thought it was just a game, though," Peter says. "When did you start getting actual messages?"

I swallow a big gulp. "Um . . . right after Grandpa died."

Peter jumps up. "Oh no. That is too creepy, Savannah."

"It's not Grandpa," Frankie says. "Sit down, Peter."

"How do you know?"

"Yeah," Kate says. "How do you know?"

I position the Star Board between all of us. "Gut feeling."

"Grandpa has no reason to haunt us," Frankie says.

"It's never been creepy," I say.

"'Cept the time it blew open the portal window and the lamp went out!" Jolene shivers. "I didn't like that time."

"Mostly never anyway," I say. "It doesn't matter, the messages have been helpful, so whatever the reason, it works. And we're in the middle of a mystery we have to solve. I'll do whatever it takes."

Peter and Kate look at each other like they might be planning an escape.

"Just try once. Please?"

We all gather around and place one finger on the little paddle. "Mr. Teach, Blackbeard, we need more help. Grandpa's clues are all mixed up. Do you know what window is special on the island?"

Nothing happens. I try talking to him, convincing the ghost that it's safe to come out. After, the attic is silent except for an occasional breeze through the drafty portal window. Kate glances at it a couple of times, probably hoping it's not going to fling open.

"Maybe we have to set up the candles," Jolene whispers. "And put on the costumes."

I shake my head. I know the ghost will show if he wants to; he showed up at the campground.

Peter clears his throat. "Excuse me, Mr. Beard, sir . . ."

Jolene giggles.

"It's not funny, Peter," I scold. "He'll never show if you make fun of him. His real name is Edward Teach."

Peter sits back, taking his finger off the paddle. "Sav, this is goofy," he says.

"It is not!" I also sit back. "That day at the campground, you saw it. 'A storm brews.' Tell him, Frankie! Tell him how it's worked."

Frankie rubs her face and sighs.

"It's real, Peter," Jolene shouts. "It's not goofy! Sometimes it just takes a while."

"Okay, One-Eyed Wonder."

"Y'all?" Kate says quietly. But we keep arguing.

"I would never make up something so serious," I say. "Grandpa left us a trail, but the ghost has given us these weird hints too. I told you, 'the brothers lose.' I didn't make that up. How could I? I don't even know what it means!"

"Guys?" Kate says a little louder over our talking.

"Savannah, you're *always* making things up," Peter says. "Why would this be any different?"

"I'm not making it up!" I look at Frankie. "Tell him I'm not making it up."

Frankie shrugs. "I don't even know anymore." Great help, she is.

"*Hello?*" Kate shouts now. "Dare family! Are any of you even seeing this?"

We all look at Kate. She seems terrified. There's a scratching noise coming from the Star Board. Only Kate's finger is still on the paddle. And it's moving. "Write it down, Savvy," she whispers to me. "Hurry up!"

I grab the pencil and paper and write down each constellation as it passes over them. It's on kind of a loop, repeating its message over and over. "Okay, okay, I got it. You can let go."

Kate whips her hand away as if the Star Board were hot and wipes her hands on her jeans. The paddle is motionless. It takes me a minute to figure out all the letters and then I read it out loud.

"Inside his wall."

"Huh?" Peter says. "What does that mean? Whose wall?"

I look around the attic, wondering if something is hidden behind *our* walls. "I have no idea."

"What are all the messages so far?" Kate asks.

" 'A storm brews,' 'the brothers lose.' And now 'inside his wall.' "

"Sounds like a poem," Jolene says.

"Yes, it does. But I don't get it."

"Sounds made-up, if you ask me." Peter stands up and examines the new map. "Poetry never makes sense anyway."

Frankie gathers our plates and takes them back downstairs while we stare at the new map.

"I can't figure out what all these lines are for," I say.

"I'm not sure, but I think this is a nautical chart," Peter says. "My dad and Robbie use them sometimes for long fishing trips. I bet they could tell us how to read this or at least what it's for."

"I don't know," I say. "I think your dad is angry at me. He might not want to help."

"He's not angry at you exactly; he's just tired of us getting into trouble together. I'll ask Robbie, instead," Peter says. "In fact, if we all ask him together, he'll be less likely to say no."

"We can do that," Kate says. Peter smiles and looks at the floor.

"Perfect. Monday after school, we will talk to Robbie about this chart," I say.

"Sounds like a good plan," Frankie says from the doorway.

"I hope so," I say. "'Cause it's the only one we got."

20 Dead in the Water

Robbie does not think it's a plan, however. We corner him by his locker at school after the last bell before he runs off to work. "What's in it for me?" he asks, slicking his hair back.

"I was afraid you'd ask that," Peter says. We already know Robbie is never going to believe anything we say about the treasure or the *Queen Anne's Revenge*. "What do you want in exchange?"

Robbie slams his locker. "I'll think about that and have my secretary get back to you."

"You have a secretary?" Jolene asks, looking amazed.

"We don't have any time to wait." I put an arm out and block him from leaving. "Just tell us what this chart is for and we'll do whatever you want when you figure it out."

Robbie looks at Peter. "Could our family get any weirder?" But he takes the map and studies it for about one minute. "It's a nautical chart for down near Cape Lookout." He hands it back. "I'll let you know my fee later." And then he leaves.

"Cape Lookout?" Frankie says, her eyebrows squeezed together.

"What's that?" Jolene asks.

"It's south of here," Frankie says. "But I don't understand. Grandpa set up our hunt here, on Ocracoke. Are you sure Robbie's telling the truth, Peter?"

"He did figure that out awfully fast," I say.

Peter shrugs. "He's always out on the boat with Dad. I hate to say it, but he's pretty smart when it comes to that stuff."

"How would we even get there? Cape Lookout is so far," Frankie says. She sounds lost. I really don't like it when my sister doesn't sound confident. "We'd need a boat."

"Cape Lookout," Jolene says, and laughs. "Get it?"

"Get what?" I ask.

"Maybe that's the window. Get it? You 'look out' a window!"

Kate's mouth drops open. Frankie and I look at each other.

I shake my head. No way. No *way* my six-year-old sister just cracked this whole thing. "That's too easy. And also too hard." I adjust my backpack and we all head outside to the bike rack to pick up our boards. Peter jogs alongside us as we skate home.

"But Grandpa's tricky," Jolene says. "'Elbow' was a branch, 'short' is a name, so why can't 'window' be a place. Cape Lookout?"

"She's got a point," Kate says.

"Do you think he'd actually send you off Ocracoke?" Peter asks. "I think Savvy's right, too easy *and* too hard."

"What do you think, Frankie?" I ask. "Do you think we have to go to Cape Lookout?"

"I think something's still missing," Frankie says. "What's linking all these clues together?" She slows down a little bit because up ahead Ryan is standing in the street waving to her. For a minute, I think she's going to turn around and go a different way, but instead, she skates right by him as he calls out. We all follow her lead.

"Hey, Frankie, wait up!" Ryan says. "Can we talk for a minute?"

Frankie skates faster. "Sorry! Kinda in a hurry!"

"I'm really sorry about the other day," he says. "I never meant to hurt your feelings. I don't believe what those girls said about your family."

Frankie stops and tells us not to wait for her.

"Are you sure?" I ask, and make two big fists. "I can make him go away."

Frankie smiles. "I can take care of myself, but thanks. I'll be right behind you. Just cover for me, okay?"

"Sure." I watch as she hops off her board and walks with Ryan down another street. We're not grounded anymore but I doubt Mom would be happy if Frankie's out super late the first day of our freedom, especially because they said no going anywhere alone.

To Peter, Kate, and Jolene, I say, "Let's go to Springer's Point for a little while." Maybe if I sit in the park, where I feel closest to Grandpa, I can make sense of some of these clues and find the missing link.

Peter and Kate look uncomfortable for a minute.

"What?" I ask them.

"We had already talked about going out on the boat, is all," Peter says. "My dad got it repaired and said we could go with him on a test drive." He looks at the ground. "And I invited Kate."

Kate blushes. "Well, I mean, Savvy and Jolene can come too, right? They're your cousins."

Peter looks stricken. I can tell Uncle Randy didn't invite us, cousins or not. I also know Uncle Randy was angry about not having enough money to fix his boat, so it makes me wonder how he got it. "Nah," I say, waving them away. "Y'all have fun. Jolene and I will think about how to crack this code." I swallow back a knot in my throat to keep myself from crying. "Jolene, we could even get that metal detector out finally, what do you say?"

"Oh really?" Jolene jumps up and down. "Savvy, yes, please, please, please! Let's do that!"

At least someone wants to hunt for treasure with me. Even if she is only six years old.

The Brothers Lose

Jolene and I mess around with the metal detector for an hour or so. It's really easy to use. All you have to do is turn it on and slowly walk around, sort of gently waving the base back and forth over the ground until it starts beeping, which is how it tells you you've found something metallic. It's a little heavy, so I hold one end and Jolene helps prop it up as we walk around the yard. All we find is three bottle caps, a quarter, and an old fishing hook. Even Grandpa wouldn't consider that much of a find. I let Jolene keep the quarter and we head inside.

"Think Mom and Dad would let us take it to the beach?" Jolene asks.

"Maybe on the weekend," I say.

"Girls?" Mom calls out when she hears the door shut. "Is that you?"

"Yes, Mom!" Jolene says. "I found a quarter!"

"Oh, that's great." Mom comes out of her office. Her hair is all pulled up on top of her head and she's wearing her reading glasses. "Do me a favor and wash up. Your aunt and uncle are coming for dinner."

"Why?" I can't help myself from asking. "What's wrong?"

"Nothing's wrong, Savvy, we're just having family over."

"We never have dinner with them unless it's a funeral or there's a problem."

Mom sighs. "Lately, yes. There're no problems, sweetheart. Court is tomorrow. We want to talk about how to handle a few things before we go." She suddenly realizes Frankie isn't with us. "Where's your sister?"

"Talking to Ryan," Jolene says. So much for cover.

"Savvy, can you please go find her and tell her she has to come home?"

"I'll go too!" Jolene shouts.

"No, you'll go wash up. I don't need all three of you out there running around." Mom gently tugs one of Jolene's pigtails. "Run up and clean those sandy hands!"

Jolene salutes Mom and runs upstairs. I sigh and head back out the front door to grab my skateboard. I'm not even sure where she and Ryan went, though I have a couple of ideas. I decide to check the school playground first, but only a few little kids are there on the swing set. So I head over to Silver Lake Harbor; there are some benches there overlooking the water.

As I round the corner, a white pickup truck comes toward me and then stops. There's an emblem of a yellow anchor on the side and the word ORCA. I can't see who it is until the driver leans out the window, tips his green hat, and says, "Good evening, little lass. What a surprise."

Throop.

I freeze. I can't really believe he's here, stopped in the middle of the road in broad daylight! I can't even move.

"You look like you've seen a ghost," he says.

"You . . . you shouldn't be here!" I finally manage to spit out. "If the police see you, they'll arrest you."

Throop laughs. "Oh, the imaginations of children. If that were the case, do you think I'd be able to take your parents to court tomorrow?"

He has a point. Had he been hanging around town all this time and nobody cared? I had seen him at Hatteras and we all saw him at the cemetery. Maybe he wasn't sneaking around. Maybe he was off the hook. Regardless, I don't need to be anywhere near him at all. I start to skate off.

"Wait one minute, Savannah! I'm actually really glad we ran into each other." Throop ducks back inside his truck and retrieves a small white envelope. "This is for you. I was going to stick it in your mailbox, but since you're here—"

"I'm not taking anything from you!"

"Trust me. You and your sisters will want to see this."

He waves it around a little bit. "It's a letter from your grandfather. Well, a copy."

"For me?"

"No, it was for me, but I think you'll find it interesting."

Everything inside my head says taking something from Throop would go against every warning my parents have ever told me. But there's a tiny other part of me that simply cannot resist something that Grandpa might have written—if Throop is telling me the truth. And the only way I will know is if I take it. I reach out, hesitant at first, and then quickly grab it out of his hand and move back.

"Savvy!" A voice calls to me from down the road. I look over and it's Frankie and Ryan heading my way. Throop drives off before I can even look back up at him. His white truck zooms off around the corner and disappears. I quickly fold the envelope and tuck it into the back pocket of my jeans. I don't want Ryan to see whatever it is. I can share it with Frankie later.

"Who was that?" Frankie asks when she reaches me.

I hesitate for a second. "Um. Someone looking for directions."

Frankie looks like she doesn't quite believe me.

"So, Mom wants you to come home now," I tell Frankie, but look at Ryan. "We're having dinner with *family*."

Ryan puts up his hands. "No problem. I'll see you at school, Frankie."

She smiles. "Okay. See you." She sort of bounces on her toes as he turns and heads away. Then she looks at me. "You're a terrible liar, Savvy. Who was that for real?"

I take a deep breath and pull the envelope out from my pocket. "It was Throop . . . Just wait! Don't freak out. He said this was a letter Grandpa wrote to him."

Frankie looks as confused as I am. "What?"

I tear open the envelope and unfold the paper, and we read it together.

April 1990

Dear Dunmore,

As you know, dissolving our partnership has not been an easy decision for me. I would much rather you come to your senses and realize that this is not a treasure to be used for one's own profit. There is value far above gold in this find and you are well aware of the personal connection I have to this mission. I will never understand your desire to fight me on this one, as we have spent so many years treasure hunting together, nor will I relinquish the ring to you. And be forewarned, should anything happen to me or the map, my sons have promised they will carry on this quest as their ancestors did before them. I will not let you tarnish the Dare name with your greed and insolent demands. I would call a parley, but then again, we both already know you are beyond the effort.

~Cornelius Franklin Dare

"Wow," I say. "Grandpa was *mad*."

"Wait, wait, wait." Frankie rubs her forehead and squeezes her eyes tight. "Just wait one second! Dad and Uncle Randy have known *all this time* that Grandpa was looking for the *Queen Anne's Revenge*?"

"What makes you say that?"

She points to the paper and reads: ". . . my sons have promised they will carry on this quest . . ."

My stomach feels tight and an awful sour taste rises up in my throat. I shake my head. "No way. No way! That would mean Dad has been lying to us about everything? He would never do that." But the proof is in my hand. It's Grandpa's handwriting. It's stuff only he knew. And obviously Throop too.

"Not to mention they clearly never promised Grandpa that," Frankie says. "Or they went back on their promise."

I kick a stone down the street. It bounces a long distance and hits a telephone pole. "I'm so mad at Dad right now. This whole time he's been pretending he doesn't believe in Grandpa's treasure hunt at all? Why, Frankie? Why would he lie to us?" Tears sting my eyes.

Frankie gently scratches my shoulder. "If Grandpa actually wrote this and it's all true, I'm sure Dad had a good reason to not tell us everything, Sav. Don't cry."

"Do you think Mom knows the truth too?"

Frankie shrugs. "I guess it's possible."

I carry my board and scuff my feet on the sandy street as we walk. "Are we going to ask him about this?" I sniff.

Frankie sighs. "I don't know. What do you think?"

"I think our parents betrayed us."

"I'm not sure we should take it that far. There has to be a reason."

I stuff the letter back into the envelope, fold it up a bunch of times, and shove it into my back pocket. "I'm asking Dad the second we get home. We have to solve this once and for all." I drop my skateboard to the ground and race off to the house. Frankie jogs behind me but I beat her to the porch. Uncle Randy and Aunt Della's car is already out front, which means I have to either bring this up in front of everyone or wait until later. But when I run up the front steps, I can hear arguing inside the house. I put my finger to my lips to warn Frankie. Together we open the door a crack and listen.

Mom's angry voice is the first one we hear. "That man paid you off, Randy. Twice! It was a bribe. Why would you do that?"

"What choice did I have, Anne?"

"You could fight him, like we are," my dad says.

"This is our livelihood we're talking about. I can't just go out and teach like you. I'm a fisherman, a boat captain, Jack. This is what I do. I have to have a functional boat! Throop wanted me to butt out, so I'm out."

"So just like that!" Mom says. "Just like that you hang the rest of your family out to dry?"

"It's not that simple, Anne," Aunt Della says.

I grab Frankie's hand and slowly open the door enough for us to squeeze into the hall. I know exactly which boards are squeaky, so I show her where to step. We hide in a corner between a coat-tree and a glass cabinet full of pottery shards Grandpa had collected.

"Where's Jolene?" Frankie whispers to me. I shake my head. Maybe they sent her upstairs. Py comes running up to us and I pull her close to me as we listen to our family argue.

"Throop has too much of a case, Jack. And too much money," Aunt Della says. "We can't fight him. None of us can even afford the lawyers."

"This. Is. Our. Home," my dad says. "Our parents' home. We grew up here, Randy. Throop has just as much right to it as the Queen of England."

"He is suing you, Jack."

"He has no case!"

"And you have no deed."

There's a loud crash from the kitchen, which I think is a glass breaking, and Py goes flying out of my arms and into the living room and up the stairs. Then I see Jolene hiding on the stairs, peeking through the banister. Tears stream down her face. I elbow Frankie. Frankie mouths the words "It's okay" and sort of waves her hands to tell Jolene to calm down. Jolene nods frantically. She wipes her cheeks and grips the railing poles.

From the kitchen I hear someone sweeping up the glass. "Sorry about that," my mom says, her voice shaky. "It slipped right out of my hands."

"It's fine, hon," my dad says. "Just watch your bare feet. I got it."

There's some shuffling sounds, chairs, I think, and then Aunt Della says, "We were desperate, Jack. Without that money, your brother would never have gotten the boat fixed and without the boat, we have no job. No income. We have three boys to raise; you have to understand that."

"I do," Dad says. "Della, you know I do. But I can't take a buyout and make my family homeless. I have to fight Throop. I hope you understand that."

"But why, Jack?" Randy says, his voice lower now. "I told you we could help you find a new place; you can stay with us for a time." There's a long pause and my uncle continues. "This isn't because you actually think . . ."

"What I think is that it's time for you to go."

Frankie grabs my hand and pulls me to the stairs where Jolene is hiding before our aunt and uncle head down the hall and out the front door. Mom and Dad hug in the hall. "Where are the girls?" Dad asks into Mom's hair.

"I sent Sav out to get Frankie. Jolene's playing upstairs. I'm sure she heard all of that."

“I’ll check on her in a second,” Dad says. “I need a quick breather.” As they walk back to the kitchen, Mom says something about how she hopes they’re going about everything the right way, and we three sneak upstairs so we can pretend we didn’t hear a thing.

22 Occam's Razor

Up in the attic, Jolene sobs in Frankie's arms as Frankie tries to explain everything that just happened. I'm not even sure I understand, so I'm glad Frankie does. I slide the Star Board out and trace the constellations with my finger as my sisters talk.

"Jo, Mom and Dad will figure this out. It's all going to be okay."

"But I thought we already saved the house, and now Throop can still take it?"

"When someone sues you in court, you have to fight to prove you're right."

"But we are right! We live here!"

"I know, but it doesn't matter now." Frankie looks at me. I know she's wondering if we should tell Jolene about the letter Throop gave me. I don't know if Jolene will be more confused or if it would help. I'm not even sure how I feel about it.

Frankie takes a deep breath. "Savannah and I think Dad and Uncle Randy might already know where the *Queen Anne's Revenge* is. Or at least how to find it."

Jolene sits up straight. "Why?"

"Show her," Frankie says. I pull the letter out and Frankie reads some of it to Jolene.

Jolene takes the letter and looks at it for a long time even though she can't read all the words. "So the treasure is definitely on the ship?"

"It's possible. Or maybe this has all just been about the ship itself. To Grandpa, and to everyone, I guess, the ship would be treasure all on its own." I have to admit, though, I'm hoping that's not true, because even if we found the wreck, it's not like we could sell it to pay for our house or Mom and Dad going to court. It would be an awesome discovery, but it wouldn't make us rich. Pirate gold or silver would be so much better.

"And Dad has always known?" Jolene asks.

"Yes."

Frankie looks at me. "We think maybe. We don't know for certain."

"Shiver me timbers." Jolene's eyes suddenly get wide as she thinks this all through. "He's a scallywag?"

"No," Frankie says. "Of course not. We're not sure. We have to ask him, though."

"Let's ask the Star Board first," I say, running my hand over the bumpy map of stars Grandpa carved into the top of the board. "It's never failed us."

Frankie nods. She lights a candle. We gather around the table, each gently placing a finger on the paddle. I take a deep breath. "Mr. Teach? We're completely lost now. We really need to talk to you."

The attic is silent.

"It's us, the Dare sisters. We need your help now more than ever. If you're here, give us a sign."

"Please, Mr. Blackbeard," Jolene whispers.

Frankie closes her eyes and quietly says, "Please help us understand what is going on."

And then the paddle starts to move. I keep one hand on it while marking down each constellation it touches around the board. Like the last few messages, it's a little longer than what we used to get.

> The brothers gain all.

A little gust of wind picks up the letter off the couch and it flutters to the ground. None of us moves for a minute, but then I pick it up and think about all our messages from the ghost.

> A storm brews, the brothers lose;
> Inside his wall, the brothers gain all.

I remember all the photos of Grandpa and Dad and Uncle Randy. And Throop. And I think I finally understand. "I thought the brothers were Peter and Robbie and Will. But it's actually Dad and Uncle Randy," I say. All of a sudden I understand everything.

"Grandpa made this treasure hunt for Dad," I say. "And Uncle Randy. Not for us. At least, not originally. That letter to Throop proves Grandpa was going to hand everything down to them if Throop didn't back off."

"Okay," Frankie says. "What's the storm, and what wall?"

I pace the attic as my theory forms. "A storm brews must be their fighting all the time. They can never get along, never have."

Jolene nods. "A lot of yelling."

"Right. And if we figure out what 'inside his wall' is about, then maybe everything works out for them." I sort of laugh and say, "Leave it to Blackbeard to make things more complicated. He and Grandpa would have gotten along great."

Frankie and Jolene stare at me. I think none of us wants to believe that this was originally for Dad and Uncle Randy because we thought Grandpa set up a special thing only we sisters would understand. But in reality, he wanted to pass it to his sons. He already gave Dad the ring. The house. At some point he probably tried to give him the map.

But Dad didn't believe him.

"We were Grandpa's last hope, right before he died," I say. "He wanted us to find the treasure, or maybe the ship, for them. For Dad and Uncle Randy. Not for us. Not to save the house."

Frankie twirls her hair and looks at the floor. "I think you're right, Savvy. I think all this is really for Dad and Uncle Randy."

"So that they'll believe in Grandpa again?" Jolene asks.

I hug her tight. "Yes, Jo. And now we have to make sure it happens." I'm a little sad that this isn't just for us, but maybe it's now even more important for our whole family than I realized.

"Grandpa probably knew they'd fight over everything," Frankie says. "That's why he ended up passing everything to us, starting with the coded letter he left for Mrs. Taylor to give us. He knew we had a better chance to get to the ship before Throop, because Dad and Uncle Randy never really believed Grandpa."

I shake the letter. "But why did Throop give us this?"

Jolene crosses her arms. "Probably because he likes making everyone angry!"

"Actually, you might be right," I say. "And it worked!"

Frankie takes the letter and folds it. "What better way to throw us off the trail than to distract us by making us all mad at each other?"

"Grandpa always said we were stronger when we stuck together," I say.

"So do we show Dad or no?" Frankie asks.

"What good will it do?"

"Probably none, considering if they find out Throop hand-delivered it, it's just going to get them all wound up again." She shoves it into her pocket and I grin. It's nice having her back on my side.

We end up eating dinner almost in silence. I think both of my parents are nervous about going to court tomorrow, but I don't bring it up. Jolene taps her fork on her plate until Frankie grabs her hand to make her stop. I sneak pieces of chicken to Py.

Even our parents don't finish their dinner.

After we straighten the kitchen, I go back up to the attic to think. I concentrate on Grandpa's treasure map of Ocracoke. With a dry-erase marker on its plastic protector, I circle all the important spots: Springer's Point, where we found the key, and our house, since it's where I found the clue and chart behind his portrait. And then I circle the cemetery, since Throop clearly thinks there's something important about that Hort guy's gravestone. I draw lines connecting all three. It makes sort of a long triangle pointing south.

I spread out everything we have on the table around the map. The key, the codes, the new chart, Grandpa's letter, the sketchbook he (probably) stole from Throop that has the picture of the Elbow Tree in it. I pick up the chart and examine it. Nothing seems to be special about it. No hidden codes like the map had, no words at all.

Once, when Grandpa was helping me with some really hard math homework, he chuckled and said, "Occam's razor, Savvy."

"Huh?" I said. "What's that?"

"It means most often the solution is right in front of you and not as complicated as you think."

I tapped my pencil on the worksheet. "If it's right in front of me, how come I don't see it?"

"Because you're thinking too hard."

"Grandpa, that doesn't make any sense!"

"Sure it does. Think about when you go to the doctor. If you have a cough, the doctor will probably look in your ears and nose and treat you for a cold. She's not going to send you off right away for a brain exam."

I giggled. "That would be silly."

"Right. She has to start with the most obvious first."

I stared at my word problem. "I still don't see it."

Grandpa laughed. "You will. Let's look at something else first and come back to it."

Grandpa was right that day. I set aside the math and worked on my spelling list for a while. After dinner we came back to my problem, and I solved it in about one minute.

But this is way harder than fourth-grade homework!

It takes me forever to fall asleep. I lie in bed for a long time twisting and turning the celestial ring in my fingers and wishing Grandpa hadn't made this so hard. *Or maybe so easy*, I think.

Off to Court

The next morning is one giant rush. Rush for us to get dressed, rush to pack our lunches, rush to get out the door. "Don't forget Ms. Davis will be stopping by to check on you after school," Mom says.

"Ms. Carolina Davis?" Jolene asks.

"Yes," Mom says. "She and I have been talking a lot since the hurricane. I think she's been lonely and she offered, so I said yes. It was either her or Aunt Della, and all things considered, I chose Ms. Davis."

"Good choice," I mumble.

Kate meets us halfway to school, and Peter runs in behind us right before the morning bell. "Whew," he says. "I didn't think I was going to make it."

"Why were you late?" Kate asks.

Peter glances at me and says really fast, "Oh, just helping my dad this morning at the harbor."

"I'm not mad at you, Peter," I say. "Our parents can handle their own selves."

"Okay, good. You know I'm on your side for this court thing. Throop should not get your house."

"I understand," I say, even though on the inside I don't totally understand. If our families just worked together, we'd all be okay. "I, um, I'm going to use the restroom really quick." I turn to Kate. "Can you tell Mrs. Erickson I'll be right there?"

"Yep." Kate nods and doesn't seem to notice I'm on the verge of tears. She and Peter head into class while I walk down the hall the rest of the way and right out the back door, my eyes stinging. But I wipe my face and keep walking. I don't even go out front and get my board, I just walk in a straight line very fast and don't look back. I don't know what happens when a kid walks out of a school, but I'm willing to take the risk. This can't wait any longer. I'm going to ask Ms. Carolina Davis everything she's ever known about living next door to my grandfather.

When I knock on her door, she doesn't act like there's anything weird about a twelve-year-old being on her porch at eight thirty in the morning on a Tuesday. "Savannah Mae! What a lovely surprise. I thought I was going to see you later this afternoon." She lowers her sunglasses just a tiny bit so I can just barely see her blue eyes.

"Yes, ma'am, but this couldn't wait. May I come in?"

Ms. Davis swings the door wide for me. As my foot crosses the threshold, I think about what my sisters and friends would say if they knew I was about to enter the home of Ocracoke's most mysterious resident. "Of course!" she says. "Please do!"

And when I do, I get an incredible surprise. Ms. Carolina Davis's home is purple.

I mean purple, purple. Everywhere is purple. The walls, the furniture, the curtains. Every shade of purple you could imagine. "Wow," I say. "This is . . . purply."

She smiles big and proud. "My favorite color." She pushes her sunglasses up on the top of her head. "Would you like a glass of water?"

"Sure. Thank you." I'm so curious about why she suddenly isn't wearing her glasses, but I don't want to be rude. She hands me the water and gestures for me to sit on the purple velvet couch.

She taps her glasses. "I don't need these in here. I have a severe sensitivity to light. Gives me very bad headaches, so I wear sunglasses everywhere. But purple seems to be the cure."

"Oh," I say. "I always wondered why you wore them. My sisters and I thought maybe you were a famous celebrity in disguise." Saying it out loud now sounds silly, but Ms. Davis just laughs.

"I'm so flattered! I wish that were the truth! I'm afraid I'm not that mysterious after all." She settles down on a chair across from me. "So, Savannah, what's so important that you're missing school to come talk to an old lady?"

"Oh." My face gets hot. "Well, I was hoping you could tell me more about my grandfather. Anything that he may have told you about some of his treasure hunts."

Ms. Davis leans back and lets out a big sigh. "Oh my. Well, it's been such a long time since your grandpa and I were close pals. My memory certainly isn't as good as it used to be."

For a second, I hesitate. And then I tell her *everything*. I just blurt it all out, from the day of Grandpa's funeral, the map he left us, the codes and key and charts we've found since, Dunmore Throop and the night at the beach. Everything. As I talk, Ms. Davis puts together a plate of cookies and brings it over to me. She seems enraptured the entire time. When I'm finished, she fans herself with a magazine.

"Well, I'll be! Sure as God made little green apples, I've never heard a more adventurous tale!" Ms. Davis takes a cookie, so I do the same.

"I suppose it is pretty adventurous," I say. "It's also been frustrating and sometimes sad."

"You miss your grandpa a lot, I'm sure. I know the two of you were close."

I look at my cookie and nod. *The closest.* Every time someone says something like that, it feels a little bit like a hole opens back up inside my chest. It hurts, but it's not entirely bad because it also makes me remember how much I love him. And that will never change. And I realize I can be sad and okay at the same time.

Ms. Davis looks at me kindly. She sits back in her chair and folds her hands. "I wish I knew more to help you girls. Cornelius told me a lot of his adventures, but he was pretty private about this one."

"It's okay," I say. "I just thought I'd ask because one of the books you had was part of it." I feel better just telling her everything, even if she can't help.

"I think your grandpa just forgot I had it, to be honest, dear. From what your parents said, his memory wasn't working so well in those last months. The only thing that rings a bell in this old head of mine is your comment about the riddles. Cornelius loved riddles; I do remember that. And you said you still haven't figured out the window—what it might stand for?"

"That's right." Other than Jolene's idea about Cape Lookout, which was a pretty good one.

"I don't know if it means anything at all, but that little portal window in your attic was handmade by your grandfather. I remember him installing it."

My heart leaps a bit. "Really? Why would it be important, though?"

"I don't know if it's important to your quest, but he built it out of pieces of a little sailboat your grandma used to take out in the sound. She was quite a sailor, you know."

I slowly shake my head. "I had no idea."

"Oh yes! I remember her taking her boat out most weekends. All by herself, just her and the water and sunshine. Bright white boat with a blue-and-yellow sail. Years after she passed, Cornelius decided to repurpose the boat. He gave away most of it for parts, but that window is built from the wood. I thought it was just the most touching thing when he told me."

"Grandpa named our house the Queen Mary after Grandma and called the attic the crow's nest, like the lookout in a ship." But he never told me that; how would I ever have known without making friends with Ms. Davis? I wonder if Dad even knows. "Ms. Davis, thank you!"

"I don't know what I did but you're certainly welcome!"

I jump up off the couch. "I don't know yet either but if that's not the window, nothing is!" I start to head out the door and realize I still have a glass in my hand. "Oh, sorry. I'll see you later, Ms. Davis!"

"Savannah, are you going back to school?"

I stop in my tracks.

"I tell you what, in exchange for your lovely company this morning, I will call the school and tell them you're with me. But we're also going to tell your parents that you missed school, okay?"

"Deal." I grin.

Queen Mary's Captain

Mom always leaves a spare key in our little shed, so I run home, grab the key, and run straight to the attic. Py jumps all over me, happy to not be home alone. Together we walk over to the portal window and examine it, the boards squeaking under my feet. I've never really thought all that much about the window, even though it is pretty cool. It's round and has several panes of glass and wooden slats that come together in the middle. Staring at it now, I think it's actually really pretty and almost looks like a clock. Or a compass.

But you have to move a compass to make it work. I examine every inch of the window and its frame, but I don't find anything out of the ordinary. It opens and shuts as usual. There're no markings. I stare out the glass, way out at the horizon where the sky and water meet. What could possibly be important about this window?

Then I start examining all the walls. "Inside his wall," I say to Py. "Has to be a wall in our house, right?" She sneezes. Wags her tail. But she doesn't have any answers.

The attic seems bigger without my sisters in it, like I'm in the belly of a great big ship. "Grandpa, something is still missing. This can't just be Occam's razor!" Py runs over to the couch and curls up on it to go to sleep. I grab a couple of Grandpa's journals and join her. She starts snoring within minutes as I turn pages, scanning for anything that might talk about the window. It's hard not to get distracted by pages and pages of writing and sketches and little maps and charts. It would be easy to get overwhelmed because there's so much to look at and read, but I try to focus on finding a page that talks about the window.

I don't find anything.

But there is a page that has a sketch of the ring. It's labeled but doesn't explain how things work. On the next page there's an infinity symbol—like a figure eight—and it's labeled in four sections with more numbers, fall and spring equinoxes, and the summer and winter solstices. The winter solstice has a date written next to it: "Dec 21" and "14:05," which I think is in military time.

All cool stuff, but I don't know what it means. I rest my head back on the couch and stare at the rafters. I don't even realize I've fallen asleep until rain on the metal roof wakes me up.

The clock says it's only noon but the attic is dark

from the rain clouds, so I flip on a light. The room has a cozy glow and rain tapping on the roof makes me really feel like I've hunkered down in the cabin of a ship. I sit up and look at everything on the table again and I keep talking out loud. It helps me think better.

"The code from the portrait said 'ring' plus 'chart' plus 'window.'" I grab one of the costumes from our dress-up trunk: baggy pants with a big leather belt, a striped shirt, and a leather pirate hat full of feathers. Then, donning a sword, I pace the attic talking to Py, my pirate dog. She's a pretty good substitute for a parrot.

"Does that mean I'm supposed to align those three things? And if so, what does that even mean, Py?"

She watches me and tilts her head as I talk. "Why would you align a ring and a window? Grandpa, that doesn't make any sense."

After a few minutes, my stomach growls and I head downstairs to make myself a bowl of cereal. Py trots down with me. The house is so quiet; it's strange. But I have to say I don't mind it too much. It's kind of nice, like I'm in charge of everything right now. I'm the captain of the ship. I march around the house for a while shouting orders to invisible crew. "Batten down the hatches! Heave! Ho!" I put Py on the arm of the couch and say, "Walk the plank!" She jumps right off. Then a sword fight breaks out between me and a traitorous mate. And then Py and I collapse on the couch and watch TV until Frankie and Jolene come through the front door soaking wet.

"There you are!" Frankie and Jolene shout at the same time.

"What do you think you're doing?"

"Mom and Dad are going to be so mad."

"Ms. Davis called the school for me." I turn back to the TV. "I'm not in trouble."

"That's what you think," Jolene says, crossing her arms.

"Oh, cut it out, bossy pants," I say. "Mom and Dad will understand. I stayed with Ms. Davis for a while. I wasn't alone the whole time."

Frankie hauls her bookbag up onto the coffee table. "I'm not covering for you."

"I don't need you to. And thanks a lot. I'm here working hard to solve the mystery, and I got pretty far, by the way, and that's the thanks I get?"

Jolene slides up to me on the couch. "What did you solve, Savvy?"

I continue to stare at the TV. "Are you sure you want to know?"

"Please tell me!" She tugs at my elbow. "What did you discover?"

"Only what the important window is."

Jolene gasps.

I lead them both upstairs to the attic and point to the portal window. "Ms. Davis and I were talking about all kinds of things about Grandpa and she told me that Grandpa made that window from the wood of Grandma's sailboat."

"He did?" Frankie says. "I didn't know that." She walks over to it and puts a hand on the glass.

"Me either. And if we go by the cipher code I found behind the portrait, we have to align the chart and window with the ring, so I guess that's the window."

"You need that book."

Jolene and I answer in unison. "What book?"

"That book Mom has that you found the code in that led you to the portrait, obviously." Frankie looks at me like I'm stupid. "*Celestial Navigation,* by B. S. Hort? There're probably directions to using the ring in there!"

I slap a hand on my forehead. "Occam's razor!"

"What?"

"Just means I overlooked the obvious." I jump up from the couch and stomp down the stairs.

In the living room I scan the shelves for B. S. Hort. Mom said she shelved the book, so it has to be here somewhere.

Suddenly there's a knock on the door. I freeze at first, but then I remember Ms. Davis was stopping by to help with dinner. I quickly find the book and tuck it under my arm. Sure enough, our neighbor in sparkly sunglasses stands on our porch. I slide the book onto a little table in the hall.

"Hello again, darling," Ms. Davis says. "I hope you're feeling better." She has her arms full with two paper bags, one of which I take as I hold the door for her to come in. "I brought all the makings for my favorite dish, shepherd's pie. Hope you girls like mashed potatoes."

"Yes, ma'am, we do." I set the bag of groceries on the counter. "But Mom said we should have leftovers so you didn't have to cook."

"I want to cook. It's a pleasure."

"Frankie and Jolene are upstairs; do you want me to get them?"

"No, no, you three can finish your homework or do whatever it is little girls do these days. Dress up? Dolls? Darned if I know." She winks at me because she knows we have much more serious things to think about, and then she starts laying out across the counter all the food she brought. Potatoes, peas, onions, beef, carrots, and more. "I'm excited to cook for a family. I'll let you know when it's ready."

I dash back into the hall and grab the book. "Thanks, Ms. Davis! We'll be upstairs if you need us!"

In the attic, I spread the book open on the table and start searching for anything about the ring. It doesn't take long at all. Right in the index is "celestial ring." I can't believe I didn't think of this sooner. We were so stuck on the window.

"Okay," I say. "Here it says the ring works like a sundial. You have to open the ring up and have a ray of sun hit a certain part of it on a certain time and day. And then it somehow gives you a location."

"Let's see the ring." Frankie holds out her hand and I take it off and give it to her. She unfolds the ring and examines the symbols. "Where on the ring?"

"I don't know."

"What time of day?"

"I don't know; that's just what it says. Look." I point to the page.

"I believe you, Sav. We just need more information." Frankie twirls a section of her ponytail. "How does a ray of light in the window give us directions?"

"It's magic," Jolene says.

"Pretty much sounds like it to me too," Frankie says. "It has to say more . . ." She takes the book away from me.

"We just have to align it, Frankie."

"But then what? How does it tell us a location? Does it suddenly start talking?" Frankie asks.

"I don't know, but there's no sun now, so we have to try it tomorrow and hope we find out."

Frankie closes the book. "This isn't enough information."

"Right now it's all we got." I know Frankie's right; I'm just hoping it will all make more sense tomorrow.

The Whole Truth

The kitchen smells delicious as we sit down for dinner. Even though I have so many thoughts swirling in my brain, it's pretty fun eating with Ms. Davis. She tells us stories, a lot like Grandpa used to, about when she was a girl growing up on Ocracoke.

"It was certainly much quieter than it is now," she says. "And we moved away for a while, but eventually my parents wanted to come back and I've lived in this house ever since. Couldn't do life on the mainland."

"I couldn't either," Jolene says, shaking her head.

"How do you know?" I say. "You've hardly even been there."

She lifts her eye patch to get a better look at me. "I just know, me hearty, I just know."

Frankie asks Ms. Davis if she knew Grandpa and Grandma as kids.

"I sure did. We palled around a bit before I moved away." Ms. Davis chuckles. "How's the shepherd's pie, dears?"

"Delicious," Frankie says. "Thank you for making it."

Ms. Davis scoops out huge seconds for each of us. "You're very welcome. We'll save the rest for your parents, who should be home any minute."

The front door opens before she even finishes her sentence. Jolene jumps up from the table and runs to the hall. "You're home! Wait till we tell you everything!"

"Hey, angel," Dad says from the hall. He sounds tired. Frankie and I look at each other. Hopefully, that doesn't mean bad news.

Ms. Davis puts a hand on my shoulder. "Don't worry, darling, I'm sure everything went fine." She starts straightening up the kitchen and putting a few things back in her bag. "I'm going to head home now and you girls let me know if you ever need anything."

"Thanks, Ms. Davis," Frankie says.

Mom comes into the kitchen as Ms. Davis leaves, each saying hi and bye and thank you as they pass.

Then Dad walks into the kitchen hobbling like a pirate with a wooden leg, with Jolene wrapped around him, sitting on his foot. "All right, kiddo, the ride is over. You're getting too big for this. Or I'm getting too old."

"Can I go watch TV now?"

"Yes, go ahead," Mom says. "One show." Jolene runs off to the living room.

"How'd it go?" I ask once my parents are both free of her. "Did we win?"

Mom ruffles my hair. "If only it were that simple! It's not done yet. The judge said the deed must be turned in within thirty days, so for now we're basically in the same place as we were this morning, only with a new deadline."

Sounds familiar, I think. "I guess that's good then?"

Dad pulls a chair out and helps himself to some of Ms. Davis's dinner. "Well, it's not great, but it's not bad."

"Mostly frustrating, Savvy," Mom says. "Because we had to sit there all day just to be told what we already know. And we have no idea where the deed is."

"Can't you just get a copy somehow?" Frankie asks.

"That's the plan, but there's no record of it at the courthouse. It's like our house doesn't even exist, according to the state of North Carolina," Dad says. "I have no idea why my father didn't leave it in a file with every other important paper."

"Or why we didn't think of it sooner, before he passed," Mom says. "Guess we just didn't think about there ever being an issue like this. We certainly never predicted Dunmore Throop."

I start clearing off my plate in the garbage when an idea comes to me. "Maybe," I say, "Grandpa *did* know Throop would be after the house, and he hid the deed on purpose."

Dad snorts. "I don't know why he'd think *that* would help."

"Savvy has a point, Dad," Frankie says.

"I think the deed is somewhere in the house and Throop knows it," I say. "He's wanted to get inside here from the very beginning."

"We've looked everywhere, Sav," Dad says.

"The key, Dad," Frankie says. I love her for bringing it up first. "It has to go to something."

Dad sighs a long, tired sigh. I can tell he just wants all this to be over. But I have to tell him one last thing. I have to try.

"Also." I take a deep breath and talk fast. "I think the *Queen Anne's Revenge* is down by Cape Lookout. And I think we have to go find it as a family."

"Savannah. This is not important right now."

"It is important! We have to try!"

"There is so much going on, and besides, how do you expect us to get to a shipwreck?"

"With Uncle Randy's boat!"

"Do you even understand how big the ocean is?" Dad says.

I cross my arms. "Yes, I do. And I also know how to find the exact location."

"You think," Frankie corrects. "You don't know."

"I'm positive," I say, even though I'm not positive. "It's the ring, Dad. You had it all along and it's the key to finding the exact location."

Dad drops his head on his arms on the table. "Savannah Mae, I . . ."

Mom rubs Dad's shoulders. "Jack, just hear her out. Has she been wrong?"

He looks up at Mom and wearily says, "Might I remind you of the lighthouse stunt?"

"Okay, other than that. Let's just listen." Mom pulls up a chair to the table and faces me. "She always understood how Cornelius thought. She might be on to something."

Dad looks sad when he hears Grandpa's name. "Even so, this is completely impractical, just like my father. He was always on some hunt or another, never dealing with the actually important things. He left that all to fall on my mom."

I've never heard Dad talk like this about my grandparents. I'm not sure what to say. Fortunately, Mom does. "Jack, let your daughter speak."

Dad finally turns and looks at me, although he doesn't look convinced. "I'm sorry, Savannah. Tell me your idea."

So I do. I tell them all the things we've found and interpreted, the ghost's messages—which Dad sort of rolls his eyes at and looks just like Frankie—and about the *Celestial Navigation* book. "I think if we align the ring with the window, it will reveal the location."

For a while, Dad just stares at me.

"What?" I ask.

"I never told anyone this before, but when I was

around eighteen, Grandpa tried to get me to go along with him on a trip to Cape Lookout. To find a sunken ship. I wasn't interested in tracking down a rumored shipwreck and I said no."

"Jack, I never knew this," Mom says.

"Like I said, I never told anyone. But yes, I knew what he was looking for. I always felt he was wasting his time. That none of it mattered. And yes, your uncle knew as well. His response was just that our father was 'crazy,' which is not true, and they didn't talk for months. Randy moved out at seventeen because of it. And when I was that age, I was more interested in getting off this island than finding some dumb pirate ship."

Frankie looks at the table. "Do you still want to get off it?" she asks quietly.

"No. I promise you, no. Nothing could be further from the truth. I was a teenager and felt like there was nothing to do here and a whole big world to explore. Which is true, there is a whole big world to explore, but I love it here now. It took me coming back as an adult to feel that way. It took your mother, and you girls. I wouldn't have wanted to raise you anywhere else in the world."

"So Grandpa went to Cape Lookout alone?" I ask. It hurts my heart to even think that both of Grandpa's sons deserted him.

Dad sighs. "No."

I slap the table. "He took Dunmore Throop!"

Dad nods. "That's when the partnership really took off. They'd known each other in the treasure-hunting world for years, but that was when they became best friends. Throop became like a son to him. I left Ocracoke for college and never looked back. And never had any idea what the two of them were doing after that. Obviously, they had their own falling out and the wreck was never found."

Everything feels heavy on my body. The letter Throop gave me is true. Frankie looks at me like she's saying she's sorry, even though it's not her fault.

Dad puts both hands on the table. "Girls, I really want to help you do this. I do. And I do believe that Grandpa has some kind of special end to this hunt for you, but right now between your uncle and the courts, we have to focus on finding the deed. Our home and future depend on it."

"But Dad—"

"Savvy, no buts. If Blackbeard's ship is out there, it's been there for nearly three hundred years and it's not going anywhere. It will be there for us when we're ready."

I slump in my chair, rolling the ring between my fingers. I don't bother to say, *I'm ready now*. Because it's pretty clear my dad does not care.

"Okay, one *but*," Dad says. "A compromise, okay?"

I sit up and glance at Frankie. She looks hopeful.

"You can stay home from school tomorrow to test your ring theory out."

I clasp my hands together. "Really?"

Mom smiles. "I'll be here if anyone needs anything, but I doubt you'll need my help."

I jump up and give them both a huge hug. "Thank you, thank you, thank you! You're the best parents in the entire world. If we figure this out, then can we ask Uncle Randy to use his boat?"

"We'll see," Dad says. "One thing at a time, okay?"

26 Hornswoggled

Once a year, every Christmas Eve, Frankie lets me and Jolene have a sleepover in her room. It's our favorite night of the year. We bring in our sleeping bags and pillows, and Frankie plays music and puts pretty scarves over the lights to make the room colorful. And we stay up as late as we possibly can to try to help Jolene see Santa.

For the first time in my entire life, Frankie decides October 29 can also be a sleepover night. Just this once.

Jolene and I race to our rooms to get our things, wash up for bed, and meet Frankie in her room before she's even changed into her pajamas. "Geez, you two are fast."

"You have to tell me everything!" Jolene says. "I never should have gone to watch TV!"

"You didn't miss much," I say as I unroll my sleeping bag. I catch her up on the important parts and leave out all the stuff about Dad and Grandpa. We can tell her about that when she's older. "And hopefully, Uncle Randy will help us once he sees what the ring can do."

But as I stare at the ceiling late into the night, after Jolene and Frankie fall quiet, I worry he will actually be really hard to convince because he's said no his whole life. Uncle Randy never cared all that much for the stuff Grandpa did, the treasures he found. I guess my dad has mixed feelings about it too. Am I the only one who truly loves it all, I wonder?

"Frankie," I whisper. "Are you awake?"

There's a soft shift of blankets. "No," she mumbles. "Go to sleep."

"Frankie, I just have one question."

"Savvy, what?"

"What do you think Grandma Mary thought about all this? Did she like Grandpa's adventures? Did she go with him? Or was she like Dad and Uncle Randy?"

"Sav, that was more than one question."

"You met her before she died; you remember her better."

Frankie sits up in bed; I can see her dark silhouette. "I only met her once or twice and I was really little. I don't remember much."

"Do you think she believed in him?"

"She took tons of photos of him, painted his portrait. He named the house after her. I'd like to think they were together on all this." She lies back down. "Go to sleep, Savannah."

That night I dream of Grandpa and Grandma sailing a ship with giant white billowing sails on a rocky, rolling sea. When I wake up the next morning, the rum song he liked to sing is in my head. I throw the sleeping bag off, grinning.

"Wake up!" I call out to my sisters. "Today's the day!"

Frankie groans. "I knew it was a mistake to let you sleep in here."

Jolene yawns.

But I get up and run up to the attic. Unfortunately, there is no sun coming through the window yet, so I go downstairs, where I find Mom drinking her coffee at the big island counter in the middle of the kitchen. She slowly turns the pages of a worn book and examines them with a magnifying glass.

"Morning, darling," she says. "I didn't think you'd be up so early when we're letting you stay home from school."

"I couldn't sleep in," I say. "Too excited." I pull a box of cereal out of the pantry, grab the milk, and make myself a bowl. "What's that?" I point to her book. "A new project?"

"No, this is one of your grandfather's journals that I think you might find helpful."

I slurp cereal off my spoon. "Why?"

She lifts the book and shows me a diagram. "I'm pretty sure these are sketches of the *Queen Anne's Revenge*."

My spoon clatters in the bowl when I drop it. "Where did you get that?" I go over and look at the pages with her.

Mom looks a little guilty. "Remember after the funeral when we were all taking some of Grandpa's things to remember him by? Well, I wanted something too. And I remembered this old sketchbook he had in his desk, filled with diagrams and simple drawings of old ships. I have no idea where he got it; I just always thought it was beautiful, but it occurred to me late last night that the *QAR* might be in it." She hands me the magnifying glass. "Look carefully at these two pages."

One page is a sketch of a full ship. The other page is a sketch of what looks like a bunch of strange shapes spread out over a grid. "A shipwreck?"

Mom grins. "I think so!"

Using the glass, I examine the shipwreck drawing. Parts of it are labeled with teeny-tiny numbers although there's nothing that shows what they mean. "No key for the numbers?"

Mom shakes her head. "Not in this book anyway. Totally your grandpa's style."

"It is, but Mom, this isn't Grandpa's handwriting." I flip a few pages. "His was curly; this is more slanted and pointy."

"Hmm, let me see." She turns the book around to look closer. "Interesting. I wouldn't have noticed that. I just assumed it was his."

I don't mention that weeks ago we found a journal that belonged to Throop that had the Elbow Tree sketch in it. That's how we found the key. It's possible this might be Throop's as well, which worries me.

Mom squeezes my shoulders as she gets up from the table. "Now you're even getting me all excited for this! We're getting closer! But first, breakfast."

"Yeah," I say as I page to the beginning of the journal to see if I can find Throop's name anywhere. It seems older than some of Grandpa's other things; the pages are yellowed, crinkly. In some places the ink is so faded you can't read it. Then, at the very end, bottom of the last page, I find it. But it's not the signature I thought.

Benjamin S. Hort.

I nearly spit out my cereal. "Mom! This was Hort's!"

"That guy who wrote the book we have?" She comes over to look at the page.

"Yes!" I remind her about the tombstone at the cemetery. "Grandpa must have been studying this sketch, which means Hort must have found the shipwreck."

"I think you're right, Savvy." She smiles at me. "Finish up your breakfast."

I try to eat but I'm too excited to be hungry. "Mom?"

"Yes?"

"Do you think it's possible Grandpa didn't actually finish the treasure hunt?"

"What makes you think that?"

Tapping my spoon on the bowl, I explain the doubt that's been growing over the last few days. "There's a lot of dead ends. I know we have to find the ship, we have proof like this, and I just feel like it's out there *somewhere*. But there's no connection to all of it. It's like Grandpa got lost in the middle of his own plan."

"I suppose that's possible," Mom says. "Sometimes when I'm working on a translation for a client, I have to read the entire book before I can translate a single word so that I have the full picture of the original author's intent."

"It could change the meaning of the words?"

"Well, it can change the interpretation of the meaning." She winks at me. "Think of the word 'bat.' How many meanings does it have?"

I use my fingers to count. "It's an animal and what you use in baseball."

"Right. And it's a verb—to bat. So I consider all the meanings and once I've read the piece, I understand the context and which 'bat' to use."

"So are you saying I might have chosen the wrong meaning for something?"

"Or just that you're missing it because you don't have the context yet. But sometimes you have to go with your instincts just as much as with the facts right in front of your face."

Jolene comes into the kitchen yawning. "Did the ring work yet?" she asks.

"Good morning to you too!" Mom says, scratching the top of Jolene's messy head.

"There was no sun yet, but I'm going to go check again." I jump down off my stool, put my bowl in the sink, and run back upstairs with Py at my heels. Frankie's just coming out of her room as I pass and she follows me up to the attic.

"Nothing yet?" she asks.

"No. Waiting for the sun to show up."

We walk over to the window, still in shadows, and I sit on the floor with my back against the wall. Frankie sits next to me. "What are you thinking?" she asks.

"The sun comes through all different times, right? Like if it's summer or winter, we might not have sun at the same time?"

"Yeah, days are longer or shorter depending on seasons."

I stand up and get the journal I was looking at yesterday. Flipping the pages, I sit back down with my sister. "Look at this." I show her the pages that have the drawings of the celestial ring. "This is obviously the ring unfolded. But this,"—I point to the figure-eight symbol—"it's something else and involves the seasons, which involves the sun. It might be important?"

“Let’s show it to Dad later tonight,” Frankie says. “He knows stuff like this. I mean if nothing happens with the ring today, then maybe this will help.”

I point to the labeled spot: DEC 21 14:05. “I have a feeling this date is important.”

“That’s months away,” she says.

“I know. That’s what I’m afraid of.”

An Unexpected Bounty

Frankie goes down to breakfast and I start to lay out on the floor everything we have so far. "When you're done, come back up to help!" I call out after her.

"Okay!"

Once everything is spread out, I make a list of every code and clue, every riddle, every puzzle. Chewing on the end of my pencil, I think about how all these things could be linked. I must think a lot more than I realize, because by the time Frankie returns, this time with Jolene, I've pretty much obliterated my pencil.

Frankie scowls. "Sav, that's gross."

I look at the end of my chewed-up eraser. "Sorry."

"What are you doing?" Jolene asks.

"Trying to figure out what is missing. There has to be something more here about when and how to use the ring."

Frankie studies the sketch of the ring and taps on the page. "If this date means anything, I'm sure it's the day we're supposed to align the ring with the window, don't you think?"

"I was afraid you'd say that."

"And if that's the case, we don't have a choice but to wait."

Jolene sighs and walks over to the portal window. She opens it and leans out a little bit. "I'm tired of waiting."

"Same here," I say.

"Ahoy, sunshine!" she calls out the window and into the sky. "Your presents are requested in the attic!"

"I think you mean *presence* is requested," Frankie says.

"That's what I said."

Frankie looks at me and shakes her head. "Well, like I said, we can ask Dad tonight. Maybe he'll understand this better and we won't have to wait so long."

"I guess."

I toss my pencil on the map and it rolls across the uneven floor, stopping on a warped floorboard. "Jolene, don't lean out so far."

"But I'm looking for more numbers!"

"What are you talking about?"

She brings her head back inside. "Around the window. There's a bunch of numbers."

Frankie and I scramble to our feet. Sure enough, on the very inner piece of the window frame, a place you can't see when the window is closed, are tiny numbers carved into the wood. I smack my forehead. "I never thought to look there. Jolene, I apologize for every mean thing I've ever said to you!"

"What do they mean?" Jolene asks. I get my chewed pencil and a piece of paper and start writing them down. "It's a basic cryptogram," I say. "Look. They're grouped together. Here's the first one."

5, 9, 7, 8, 20

I write out the alphabet and give each letter a number. "This is a really easy puzzle," I say. "Grandpa probably figured no one else would see it in our house except us. It's in order, so 'A' equals 'one,' 'B' equals 'two,' and so on." I write down the word.

EIGHT

Jolene leans over my paper, blocking the light. "Do the rest, Savvy!"

"I'm trying!" I slide her a piece of paper. "Here, you can help."

Together we translate all the numbers.

Eight steps across the quarterdeck

Frankie raises her hands in the air. "How does that make sense?"

"What's the quarterdeck?" Jolene asks.

"Part of a ship," I say. "I guess just part of the deck." I put my hands behind my head and pace. The boards creak under my feet. Py follows me back and forth. "He doesn't mean the *QAR*, does he? Think, Savvy, think."

"Unless," Frankie says, "you're standing on it."

"Standing on what?"

"Savvy, don't you see? The house is named the Queen Mary. Grandpa always called this the crow's nest. We are *on* the ship. We always have been."

Jolene clasps her hands together and squeals.

I walk over to the window and then turn around. "Eight steps across the quarterdeck." We count each board as I walk until I reach the eighth. The squeakiest one. Frankie rushes to me and I crouch as we try to move the board. It gives a little bit, but we can't pry it up. "We need a knife," Frankie says. "Where's Grandpa's knife?"

"You never gave it back to me after that day we made a blood promise to find the treasure." I cross my arms and pretend I'm angry even though I totally forgot she had it.

"Oh, that's right." She jumps up. "I'll be right back!"

She's back in less than a minute and slides the blade between the boards. "Ready? I'm going to pry, but you have to try to grab the wood."

"Okay," I say. "Go."

The board squeaks and groans as it releases from the other boards. I grab it and Jolene helps and we pull the whole thing up. It's only a section of the longer floorboard and sort of pops out of place. A dark, cobwebby hole is left.

Frankie closes the knife and lets me have it back.

"Flashlight?" she asks.

"Nah." I plunge my hand into the darkness, cobwebs, dust, and all, until my fingers hit a metal box. It feels like sparks fly through my body. "This could be it," I whisper. "This could be Blackbeard's treasure."

"Pull it out!" Frankie says.

I press my hand firmly on the box. "Let me savor this minute and commune with the pirates who came before us."

"Savannah Dare!"

I grin and pull the metal box out of the floor. It's heavy, but it doesn't make any noise. But it's intricate and old and certainly looks like it could have had treasure in it at some time.

"Is it locked?" Jolene asks. "Is that what the key is for?"

"I don't know." I try to unlatch it and at first it seems locked, but then suddenly it gives and the lid pops open. "I guess not."

Inside is a pile of papers. It's hard to hide my disappointment. "That's it?"

Frankie gently picks them up. "Let's see what they are." She unfolds the top one and it's Grandpa and Grandma's marriage certificate. Two more are Dad's and Uncle Randy's birth certificates.

"What are these?" Jolene asks.

"Just grown-up papers," I tell her. "Not treasure. I don't know why they're in here."

"Wait a minute," Frankie says as she unfolds several pieces of paper. "I think this is the deed Mom and Dad have been looking for!"

"Frankie, I think you're right!"

She jumps ups. "We have to show them!"

"Wait, let's see what the rest are." The next folded piece is much larger and I gently unfold each layer until we have it fully spread out on the floor.

"Another map?" Jolene asks.

"Yes." I look closer. "Or no. I think it's the same one I found behind the portrait. Look."

Frankie turns it so she can see it better. "This one has different marks."

I grab the original chart and the new chart and compare them. Definitely the same chart but with different markings. I lay the new chart over the old one. "Frankie, can you hold these up to the light for me?"

"Sure." She stands up with the charts and holds them in front of a lamp.

Just as I expected. When all the lines are together, they form a large cross symbol and a complete set of numbers, which are coordinates, in the ocean off the coast of Cape Lookout.

Sometimes X really does mark the spot.

"I present to you: the exact location of the *Queen Anne's Revenge*."

Frankie has the biggest smile and Jolene claps her hands. Grandpa would be so proud of us.

"We don't have to align the ring with the sun because Grandpa already did the work," I say. "He made sure everything was covered!"

"What's this last one, then?" Jolene asks. I'm so mesmerized by the charts I don't even look over. "Savvy? Frankie? I can't read all these words."

"Just hang on, Jolene, I'm thinking. We're still going to have to figure out how to get out there." I trace the route with my finger. It's so far away.

"Uncle Randy?" Frankie suggests.

"He'll never agree."

Jolene sounds out letters behind us. "T-th-tach, Dare, and this is Hort, like that guy in the cemetery!"

"Let me see," Frankie says as she gently lays the charts on the table. "Wow, Jo, be careful. That looks really old."

The paper Jolene holds looks so old it might tear if she breathes on it too hard. "What is that?" I gently take it from her and lay the flimsy, yellowed, tissue-like sheet flat on the floor. It's a handwritten flow chart with intricate, little, decorated boxes of names that lead to more names. "Drummond." "Hort." "Thatch." "Teach." "Dare."

"Frankie, what is this?"

She looks over my shoulder. "I think it's a family tree. See?" She points to a name in a bottom box. "Cornelius Franklin Dare. It's . . . our family tree."

"But Drummond, Thatch, Teach . . . those are names Blackbeard used." I trace my finger from the top box to the one with my grandfather's name in it. "Grandpa is a descendant of Blackbeard?" I whisper, staring at Frankie. "We, the Dare family, are descendants of Blackbeard?" Saying it out loud makes my heart and head pound—in a good way. Everything is spinning and sparkling and I can hardly think. Both of my sisters stare wide-eyed at me.

I stand up and shout, "We're pirates!"

A Battle of Wills

"Is it really, really real?" Jolene asks. "We're really pirates, Savvy?"

"I don't think Grandpa would have taken so much effort to hide this if it wasn't real."

"We're not pirates!" Frankie says. "Pirate does not get passed down in your DNA."

"Whatever," I say. "Close enough for me." Grinning, I gently pick up the family tree. "We have to show this stuff to Mom and Dad. It's all the proof we need."

Frankie holds up a hand. "Leave it spread out on the floor. It's too fragile. I'll go get Mom." She scrambles up off the floor and runs out.

"Jolene, it's a good thing you found that code. You saved us."

Jolene smiles. "Aye-aye, matey." I give her a huge hug.

Frankie and Mom return to the attic and at first she

seems shocked there's a hole in the floor but then we show her everything we found. After that, it's a big blur. Mom is thrilled we found the deed and shocked about the family tree, and all of us have to wait until Dad gets home to show him too. While we wait, Mom works at securing the family tree onto a piece of cardboard so it doesn't tear.

When Dad finally comes in the door, we kind of all attack him. Everyone talks at once and even Py barks at him until he holds up his hands. "I surrender!"

"You're going to want to sit down, honey," Mom says, ushering him to the living room. "I didn't believe it at first, but, well, just wait. Savvy, Frankie, bring everything in here."

We parade each piece in, one by one, showing Dad what we found. His mouth drops open wider with each discovery but he seems to be lost for words. He scratches his chin and squints when he sees the family tree. "No way." He looks at Mom. "That can't be real."

"Looks pretty authentic to me, Jack. And it clears up why Throop was so dead set on getting this house. He had to have known all these documents were in here somewhere, the charts especially."

"Can I invite Peter over?" I ask. "Please?"

Dad nods but looks dazed. "Yeah, yes, of course. Invite the whole family. They need to see this too."

Once my aunt and uncle and cousins arrive, for the rest of the evening, my entire family sits in the dining room with all the documents spread out across the table, as well as some other books and files that belonged to Grandpa. Little Will sits with the adults while Aunt Della gives him a snack. Mom makes coffee and they seem to be settling in for a long while, so me and my sisters and Peter sit on the couch talking about what they could possibly still be going over.

"The facts are plain and simple," Peter says.

"Aye!" Jolene says. "We're pirates."

"We're *not* pirates," Frankie says, and points at all three of us. "None of you can go around saying that."

She's right, but I like to think I'm closer to being a pirate than your average twelve-year-old. How many people get to claim Blackbeard as a great-great-however-many-greats grandfather? I start pacing the room, thinking about how we're going to get to that shipwreck if Uncle Randy won't take us.

"Fine," Jolene says. "We're ascendants."

Peter laughs. "*De*-scendants."

"That's what I said."

"Savvy, what's the matter?" Frankie asks.

"I'm just anxious about getting to the *Queen Anne's Revenge*."

"It's not like we can go anywhere today," Frankie says. "It probably takes a whole day just to get there."

"I know, but we could start planning. We could look at the chart together and decide when to go. They haven't even discussed that part yet."

"I think right now they're more worried about the deed," Peter says. "Besides, now that you have everything, Throop will never get to it. You won!"

Suddenly there's a knock on the door. Jolene jumps up. "I'll get it!" We can't see her but we hear the door open and she yells. "It's Kate!" We all jump up then and rush to meet her.

"Oh!" She steps back a bit. "Hi, everyone. Savvy, I brought you your homework." She hands me a textbook with paper sticking out. "Mr. Baranski asked me if I was able to get it to you and I said sure! Mom made me wait until after dinner. You don't look sick, though—"

Jolene grabs Kate's hand. "You're never going to believe—" Jo looks at me and Frankie. "Can we tell her?"

We all sort of gently push Kate out to the porch, where we sit and tell her about the day's discovery. Her face lights up more and more with each part. "This is incredible! I want to go with you!"

"We don't even know if we're going to go," I say. "We're waiting on all of them to decide. And it doesn't sound like they're convinced we're right about everything."

"My dad is still pretty against it," Peter says, frowning.

Kate thinks for a minute. "Well, if he doesn't want to take you, can't Robbie?"

"He'd probably be even less likely than my dad," Peter says.

"I don't know, Peter. I bet we could convince Robbie quicker than Uncle Randy," Frankie says. "Look how quickly he helped us with the chart. He can be grumpy, but I bet he'd do it. It's a good idea, Kate."

"It's a great idea," I say. "But let's try Uncle Randy first. With all of us together, all that proof, plus Mom and Dad, how could he say no?"

But when we approach the adults at the table and propose our plan, Uncle Randy says, "No."

Peter looks at me with a *I told you so* look.

"Randy," Dad says. "Let's sit on all this for a while, get through the trial, which will be a cinch now, and maybe in a few weeks we could take a weekend and just go explore a little bit. For the kids' sake."

Uncle Randy taps his finger on the table as he looks at all of us. "I admire your determination, but even if this is real, it's not like we can haul up a shipwreck. Your girls haven't even learned to dive yet. There is no point. I think these charts should be turned over to the proper authorities. Let them deal with it."

"But if there's treasure on the ship, it belongs to us!" Jolene says.

Uncle Randy covers his face and then looks at us. "There's no treasure on that ship! And if there was, you have no way to get it."

"But *you* can dive," I say. "Robbie can too. You could teach us."

"This is getting so out of hand." Uncle Randy stands up. "I'm glad you girls found all these things, that your little treasure hunt wasn't all for nothing, but as far as I'm concerned, the biggest win is that you saved the house. Again. Throop has no chance now. You should be grateful for that. End of story."

I stomp my foot. "It is *not* the end of the story! Do you have any idea how hard we've worked to get this far?"

"Savannah," my mother warns.

"Mom, it's not fair!"

My aunt and uncle start getting ready to leave. "It's not about being fair, Savannah," Aunt Della says as she packs up little Will's toys. "It's about being practical."

"Being practical never got anyone anything."

"Well, being foolish will only bring you trouble. And you've had a fair share of it," Uncle Randy says. "Your entire life has been nothing but getting yourself into trouble. Trouble at school, roaming around on your own, always dirty."

My dad steps up. "Now, Randy, that's enough."

"You spoil that kid too much," Uncle Randy says. "You're going to regret it when she's a teenager."

I cross my arms and clench my teeth and try really hard not to cry. But Uncle Randy's words are the meanest yet. I try to remember what Grandpa used to say about kids who teased me and how it often meant they were jealous or didn't understand and that made them fearful. And fear can make people angry. But it doesn't help this time. I'm so mad I want to think up the meanest, most hurtful thing I can say back, but there are no words. Instead, I run out of the house and into the night and ignore my mother's call to stop.

Crafting the Perfect Plan

I run so fast I don't realize until I'm almost at the light-house that Frankie and Kate followed me. "Savvy, can you please just stop?" Kate calls, out of breath. "Please!"

When I reach the fence that goes around the light-house park, I lean against it to catch my breath and wipe my face before they catch up to me.

Frankie hugs me as soon as she reaches me. "He had no right to say all that."

"It's all true, though," I say into Frankie's shoulder. "I am dirty all the time. And I do get into trouble."

"So what?" she says. "You can get clean and you're an incredible treasure hunter. Look at all the codes and puzzles you can solve. Uncle Randy is just jealous you're smarter than he is."

That makes me laugh. I pull away from Frankie. "You really think so?"

"I do."

Kate puts her arm around me. "I think you're the most interesting person I know."

"Thanks." I smile at her. "Are you going to get into trouble being out here so late?"

Kate shrugs. "I'll deal with it."

"But we should head back, Savvy. Mom was worried."

"Okay."

We start walking back to the house when Peter comes flying up to us out of breath. "Hey! I'm sorry my dad was so mean back there."

"It's not your fault," I say. "I just wish he was on our side."

"I actually think he feels bad for what he said; he said I could go find you."

"What are we going to do?" I ask out loud. "We have to get a boat to take us out."

"I say we ask Robbie," Kate says. "It's the last hope."

"He's going to ask for something in return," Peter says. "I guarantee it."

"Yeah, but Kate is right. He's our only hope." Although I'm a little scared to ask Robbie, I feel lighter. Like there's still a possibility to get to the shipwreck. "Money always works, right? How much money do you all have?"

Frankie says, "We have some from the ghost stories that we could earn back in a snap if we needed to. Peter? Kate?"

"I have some birthday money left over," she says.

"Whatever you can contribute. Let's gather as much as we can find and meet at Robbie's work tomorrow after school." I put my hand in the middle of everyone. "And we have to commit to not telling another soul what we're doing. Blackbeard's family only." I look at Kate. "And one by extension."

She smiles at me. "I always wanted to be part of your family." She puts her hand on top of mine. Everyone else follows.

"Well, you are now," I say. "Tomorrow we meet on the playground and plan our attack."

The next day, we meet after school and pool our money. Frankie has four dollars, I have the money from the ghost stories, Peter has two, Jolene has a handful of coins, and Kate has ten dollars.

"Kate, that's too much!" I say.

"This is a good cause," she says, and hands me the ten. Altogether we have $22.56. How could Robbie say no?

We race to the harbor restaurant where Robbie works as a busboy cleaning off tables. Kate has gotten really good on her skateboard. She skid-stops short of hitting Peter by inches. "Wow," he says, cheeks turning pink. "You're better than Savvy now."

"Hey!" I smack his arm. "Go get your brother."

Peter goes inside and we wait for about five minutes before he comes back out with Robbie, who looks less than thrilled. "I just clocked in. What in the world do you twerps want? Somebody die?" The smell of hot oil and fried shrimp and potatoes comes out of the restaurant behind him.

Frankie rolls her eyes at our cousin but does all the talking. "We need your help. We're prepared to pay."

Robbie crosses his arms and leans against the wall. "How much?"

We pull out our money and try to hand it to him. A few pennies hit the ground.

He holds up a hand. "Never mind. Keep it. Just tell me what's so important that you all broke your piggy banks for it."

After we explain what we've been doing the last few weeks, and what Grandpa claimed to know, and especially what we found under our floorboards, his expression changes many times. From impatience to giving us a chance, he seems to warm up the more we talk. He knew a little about the fight over the house but mostly hasn't been around much to hear the whole story. Finally, when we're done, he says, "Dad always used to argue with me when I talked about this stuff."

All of us are quiet for a minute. I was prepared for a lot of possible reactions, but I don't think any of us expected this one.

"Wait," Peter says. "You've *known* about this? How is that possible?"

"I didn't really *know*. Grandpa used to tell me stories. You know, when I was like Will's age. I'd repeat stuff back to Dad and he'd yell at me for making stories up, believing imaginary things, so I stopped." Robbie looks out across the harbor. "And actually, Dad told Grandpa to stop too. Eventually I just kind of pushed it out of my mind, I guess." He checks his watch. "But what does this have to do with all the money? What do you want?"

"We need you to take us to Cape Lookout," I tell him. "That's near where the *Queen Anne's Revenge* is shipwrecked. Grandpa had the exact coordinates, and now, after a lot of work, we have them too."

Robbie looks at me like he can't quite figure me out, but he's curious. He looks at Peter.

Peter says, "Dad knows it's real but he's so stubborn. He doesn't think there's any reason to go looking because we can't do anything with it."

"Well, I mean, you'd get credit for finding a pirate ship," Robbie says. "That's pretty cool."

"Exactly!" I bounce on my feet. "So will you take us?"

Robbie looks at all of us and purses his lips together. Finally, he nods. "I have off on Saturday. We'll need to leave at dawn in order to have enough time. Bring food, a lot of it, and water. I'll take care of the rest." And then he ducks back inside the restaurant.

My heart races. I can't believe we're setting sail to find a pirate shipwreck. Kate grabs my arm and we all circle around one another and try not to jump and scream too loud with victory. I always thought Robbie hated us and didn't care all that much about Grandpa, but I guess I was wrong. I guess there's always more to the story, just like Grandpa used to say. Grandpa was right about a lot of things, and now we get to prove it by finding the *Queen Anne* for him.

30

Charting the Course

On Saturday we leave a note for our parents that says we're going fishing with Peter. They won't worry or come looking for us for at least half a day, but I'm not sure what's going to happen when lunchtime rolls around and we're still not home. I imagine they will figure out where we've gone. We all know we're probably going to end up in the biggest trouble of our lives, proving Uncle Randy right, but finding a pirate ship that belongs to our pirate ancestor feels totally worth it.

"Maybe when we come home famous they won't be able to be angry at us," I say to Frankie after we shut the front door. We go around to the shed, where we hid water bottles and sandwiches we made last night.

"I think we can pretty much count on being grounded for the next year, Savvy."

"Me too?" Jolene asks.

"Are we forcing you to go with us?"

She shakes her head. "You're not leaving me behind again!"

"Then yes, you'll be grounded too."

We walk to the harbor, where Robbie, Peter, and Kate are getting the boat ready. The sun is just starting to rise off to the east, giving us enough light to walk the dock. The salty-fish smell of the water and the boats clanking against the dock make me imagine what it would have been like to be a pirate getting ready to set sail.

We load up all the food and water, and Robbie hands everyone a life vest.

"What did you tell Uncle Randy?" I ask.

"I didn't tell him anything," Robbie says. "I'll probably get my license taken away for doing this."

Suddenly it hits me how serious it is that we're basically stealing our uncle's boat and running away by sea. Now we really are pirates. I swallow hard and tell myself we have to do this for Grandpa. And we have to do it for Dad and Uncle Randy, even though they don't know it and even if they are mad at us for the rest of our lives.

"We have to hurry up," Peter says. "Dad heads out here by seven on weekends." He winds up a long rope and tosses it on board. "Kate, can you do that one?"

Kate jumps up and repeats what Peter did. Robbie works on the controls. And my sisters and I stay seated on the bench, out of the way. It's amazing watching them prepare everything; even Kate has an idea of what to do since she went out with my cousins before. Maybe more than once by the looks of it. Uncle Randy never taught me anything on the boat.

"All right," Robbie says. "We're about ready. While you're aboard the SS *Dare,* the rules are"—he uses his fingers to count as he talks—"life vests don't come off until the boat is docked when we get back home. No one enters the wheelhouse unless invited. That's the captain's quarters. And you stay on your butt until we get out there and if I tell you to still stay on your butt out there, then you have to listen because I'm the captain."

Jolene starts to salute him but stops and squints with her one unpatched eye. "If you're captain, where's your hat?"

"It's in the wash." Robbie starts the engine and within minutes we are out of the harbor, cruising through the inlet and heading south toward the Atlantic Ocean as the sun really begins to rise to our left over the massive expanse of gray-blue water. We watch it lift out of the waves, red and orange fire across the watery horizon, almost hailing us on our way to find Blackbeard's ship. It's the most beautiful thing I've ever seen.

We tell Robbie more details about everything that's happened in the last weeks, from the map to the first coded letter from Grandpa. Turns out he knows some of it from his family talking at home, but he's completely enraptured when we tell him about how we found everything, decoding riddles and puzzles to lead to each hint.

"You were really paying attention to everything Grandpa ever said, weren't you?"

I nod. "I knew it was all real."

Robbie looks a little sad when I say that, so I add, "And my parents let Grandpa tell me all the stories. They never told him he couldn't. So, I mean, maybe it would be different for me if they had. Maybe eventually I wouldn't have believed him either." I can't imagine that, though. Grandpa would have had no one if not me. And for the longest time I didn't feel like I had anyone except Grandpa. But now? All of us cousins and even Kate, heading out to find a pirate ship together? Grandpa would be so excited and proud if he knew how we all came together to do this. I look up at the cloudless sky and think maybe, somehow, he does know.

After a couple of hours, we break out the food. I hand Robbie a peanut butter and jelly sandwich. "Perfect treasure-hunting meal," he says, half joking. But I laugh with him. Peanut butter and jelly was the only thing we had enough of. And we had to use an entire loaf of bread, which Mom is probably noticing right now.

After we eat, Robbie gives everyone a turn driving the boat. Even Jolene, who has a grin on her face like I've never seen. "Look at me, Savvy, I'm captain!"

"The captain has to keep her eyes—or eye—on the horizon," Robbie gently turns Jolene's head with his hands.

It's a long trip and I think each of us dozes off here

and there, lying on the benches in the warm, autumn sun. We talk a little bit about what to do when we find the shipwreck, because we obviously can't get it off the ocean floor ourselves. Peter suggests calling the Coast Guard, which we all agree is probably the best choice. They'll know exactly what to do. And we talk about our family and how amazed they will be once they get over being angry. Or worried. I feel a little bad about that, but I think finding the ship will make up for it.

Soon, Robbie's asking for the chart and the coordinates, which he can plug into his controls and guide the boat to. We give him everything and he says, "We're only about thirty minutes out."

My foot starts bouncing.

Frankie twirls her hair.

Jolene gets a sudden burst of energy. "Yo ho, yo ho! A pirate ship today!"

Belowdecks!

Robbie cuts the engine and we coast a little bit, rocking on the waves as he turns on the sonar. "The water is really shallow here," he says. "Are you sure those coordinates were right?"

"Positive." I point to the equipment Robbie sets up. "How will that work?"

"The sonar? It's only about thirty feet deep here and the sonar picks up anything around us, basically. We use it for finding fish to figure out where to drop nets. And we find trash all the time." He turns it on, and a bunch of numbers on the screen light up. We gather around to see how it works. Right away we can see images of the seafloor beneath us.

"Wow."

"So I'll slowly go back and forth over this area and

we'll see if it picks up anything that looks big enough to be a boat."

"And if it does?" I ask.

"Then I'll put on the dive suit and go check it out." He shrugs as if he goes looking for shipwrecks all the time.

"Robbie, thank you, thank you, thank you!" I say. "We never could have done this without you!"

"Don't get carried away. Let's see if this baby even picks up anything other than garbage."

Robbie slowly drives the boat back and forth, almost like he's mowing the lawn, long rows one way and back again. A couple of times he gets something interesting on the screen, but each bleep turns out to be too small to be a ship. It feels like hours go by. We have more snacks and try to be patient.

There's nothing but water in all directions and I daydream about what it must have been like for pirates to see nothing but water for days. A ship could surely sink and never be noticed. Maybe even completely forgotten for the rest of time. But because of people like my grandpa, sometimes legends last forever. I realize how lucky we are to be part of the story now.

But after over two hours of searching, we can't find anything. Jolene is sound asleep on one of the benches and everyone is a little wobbly from being on the water for so long.

Robbie looks at me, an apology in his eyes. "We can't stay out here much longer. It'll get dark before we get home."

"Please, just a little while longer? I know it's here somewhere," I plead. Our story can't end like this, in the same place Grandpa's did—with only a location but no treasure.

"We have a four-hour ride back." Robbie looks at his watch. "Thirty minutes more and then we have to head home."

"Deal." I lean on one of the benches and look out. I know I'm not going to see anything this way, but I can't stop staring out into the water and trying to will the *Queen Anne's Revenge* into existence. Grandpa had to be right. I want to tell the end of this story with the Dare sisters—and cousins—being the true guardians of not only Grandpa's treasures but Blackbeard's.

Frankie comes over to me. "Savvy, this might not happen today."

Tears sting my eyes. "It has to, Frankie. We will never be allowed out here again if we don't find proof. We'll be in so much trouble and Uncle Randy will hate me forever."

"Uncle Randy doesn't hate you." But she doesn't say anything else. I can feel her worry and it scares me.

"Grandpa trusted us." My throat is so tight the words come out like squeaks.

Frankie puts her arm around me. "We will get back out here eventually. I'm sure of it."

"Like when?" I ask. "Like when I'm thirty and have my own boat?"

Frankie laughs. "Maybe."

"It's not funny! It'll be too late. Throop will beat us to it. He has so much of the information already; we'd have to guard the charts with our lives forever. If not him, someone else. It has to be today."

Frankie sighs and sits down on the bench. I join her, put my head in my hands, and stare at my feet while Kate and Peter continue watching the screen with Robbie. Thirty minutes goes by very slow and very fast at the same time.

But then suddenly, an "Oh wait!" from Robbie breaks me out of my sorrow. Frankie and I jump up and join him. Kate wakes up Jolene.

"This looks like something big," Robbie says. He pushes a button to drop the anchor. We gather around the sonar and he shows us the outline of something enormous beneath us, rising out of the otherwise flat, sandy bottom. Kate grabs my hand. Goose bumps rise up all over my arms. Jolene shivers.

Frankie outlines the shapes with her finger. "This goes all the way over here, and then this section almost looks like it's all broken apart or something." She looks at Robbie. "It could be it."

Robbie nods. "It definitely wouldn't survive in one

piece. There'd be wood and cannons and stuff everywhere." Which reminds me of the sketch Grandpa had. Then he clears his throat a bit. "Or it could also be a ton of trash someone dumped. But this one is worth checking out." He looks at his watch again. "We are really cutting it close, but I have to at least take a quick look. Frankie"—he taps the screen—"write down these exact numbers. All of them. They are more accurate than the charts."

While Frankie does that, he goes to the back of the boat and changes into dive equipment, strapping things all over his body. A mask, snorkel, flippers, air tank.

"I've got to learn how to do this," I say.

Peter helps him get his oxygen tank on and guides him to the edge of the boat. "Don't stay down too long, okay? You're not supposed to dive alone."

"Aw, baby brother, are you worried?" Robbie winks at Peter and then falls backward into the gray choppy water. We all watch until he disappears completely. *It must be amazing down there,* I think. Like a whole other world. I'm so jealous I can't go with him and see it all for myself but so happy we have him.

I sit back up and look out right into the starboard side of a boat I recognize.

The *Brigantine.*

"Wow," Kate says when she looks up. "Where did that come from?"

I can hardly speak. "It . . . he must have followed

us, and we weren't paying attention." We'd been so engrossed in the sonar we never saw him coming.

"Who is it?" Kate asks.

Frankie puts her arm around me. "It's Dunmore Throop."

32

Mutiny on the SS *Dare*

Throop cuts his engine, anchors his boat, and steps out from the cabin. "Ahoy, SS *Dare*!"

None of us says a word. He's so close that any of us could jump between boats.

He squints into the sun, which is now slowly falling in the western horizon, but is still bright and hot. "You're supposed to say, 'Ahoy, *Brigantine*' back, don't you know that?" Throop sneers at us with a joyful grin. He looks like he just won the lottery.

Jolene shouts back. "Ahoy, you big—" I clamp my hand over her mouth.

To Throop, I say, "Why are you following us? You shouldn't be anywhere near us."

"Who said I was following you?" Throop folds his hands on the side of the boat and bends down like he's trying to hear us better. "I was out enjoying this beautiful blue Saturday and just happened to run into old family friends."

"Hours from home?" Frankie says sarcastically.

Throop nods toward Kate and Peter. "I see you have more help now. But who's the captain of this ship? Surely none of you drove this boat *hours from home*. And I know Randy had no interest. He was easy to pay off to butt out."

The mention of my uncle's treason makes my blood boil, but I won't let Throop know how mad I am. His eyes search the cabin, the deck, and the benches. He stops on the open bench full of dive equipment. "Ah-ha."

None of us says a word. I notice Peter scanning the water for his brother.

Throop stands up straight. "So, did you find something interesting?"

"We're fishing," Kate blurts out.

"Where are your poles?"

"We're using nets," she says.

"Hmm. Of course." Throop scratches his chin. "Where are the ropes?" He looks at the distance between our boats. "I think I better come aboard. It's not safe for young people to be out in the open ocean all alone. And it will be getting dark soon."

He begins to step across the watery divide but before he can place a foot on our boat, I slide my legs through the railing and push his boat away with my feet as hard as I can. "Don't you dare!" I yell. It sends both of our boats rocking back away from each other, and Throop stumbles backward.

Throop gets up, anger contorting his face at first, and I'm afraid he might launch himself right toward me, but then he quickly composes himself and leans against the side of his boat again. He stares right at me. "Savannah, you and your crew wouldn't be here if it wasn't for me. You might have had a couple of important facts, and my ring, but you didn't do this all by yourself."

I don't say anything. He's right that I didn't do it all myself. Some of it was his research. Some of it was Hort's. A lot was Grandpa's. And some was just dumb luck. But if he stole from Grandpa and Grandpa stole from him, maybe they were even.

Throop shrugs. "Look at it this way. We're all in it together now. Since everyone else is dead and gone, what do you say we both take credit for the find?"

Jolene picks up some kind of grappling pole, holds it like a sword, and stands up on the bench. "No way, Mr. Throop! The pirate ship belongs to the Dare family!"

"Aren't you a feisty one." Throop chuckles. "Is that so? And how do you surmise that?"

Jolene starts to tell him, but Frankie says, "Jo. Enough." She shakes her head. "Get down." Jolene closes her mouth but remains posed for a fight high on the bench.

"Without the letter I gave you, without the ring and sketchbook your grandfather stole, would you even be here?" Throop asks. "You'd still be running all over Ocracoke, spinning yarns for campground children, digging in the sand, climbing the lighthouse stairs, searching for books and codes that go nowhere."

Peter and I look at each other. Throop must have been watching us this whole time.

Peter points to Throop. "You had no right spying on us!"

"It's a free country," Throop says. "Besides, someone had to do something. You needed me and I needed you. I knew you weren't going to give up that ring. I mean no harm to any of you. I just want to claim what is rightfully mine. So here we are." Throop puts his foot on our boat again. "Let's call a parley, Savannah. Let me come aboard and we will finish this quest together."

"Grandpa wouldn't parley with you!" I reach through the railing with my leg again.

But just as I push off as hard as I can, Frankie yells, "Savvy, no!"

Annoyed, I look back at her. "What?" And then I hear the splash.

Kate and Peter run to the side. "Jolene!"

I scramble up and look over to see my little sister splashing her arms and spitting out water.

"Jolene!" I shout. "I'm so sorry!"

"I'm drownding!" she screams. Her head bobs below the gray water. Small waves crash in her face. She gets mouthful after mouthful of water because she's flailing so much. I'm frozen in place, forgetting anything I'm supposed to do right now. Completely useless.

Frankie leans over the edge to try to reach her but she's too far. "You're not drowning, Jolene. Listen to me. Stop flapping your arms. You'll float, you have a life vest on. Just relax!"

"Find the life ring!" Peter yells. It snaps me out of my frozen state. We all frantically search the boat for the red-and-white floating ring, flipping open all the benches and cabinets. Peter finally finds it tucked in the cabin behind a seat. He's about to throw it for Jolene when we realize Throop has already thrown his. Jolene holds on for dear life and we all watch as he slowly pulls her aboard the *Brigantine*.

Now I step up on the bench with a pole in my hand. "Dunmore Throop! If you harm a hair on her head, I swear I'll—"

He holds on to the back of Jolene's life jacket, keeping her steady. She coughs a little water up but looks okay. "You'll what?"

"I'll—" I have no ammunition against him. "I'll—"

"I tell you what," he says. "We can trade. Your baby sister for the charts on your boat."

"What?" I yell. "What kind of trade is that?"

"Savvy," Frankie says. "Just do it."

I turn to her. "We can't!" But even as I say it, I know we have to. He has Jolene. We have no choice. Frankie goes into the wheelhouse and brings out the charts. My chest tightens, as if I were the one underwater, holding my breath. I can't believe it's come to this. Frankie gets up on the bench with the charts in her hands.

"Let her go, and I'll hand you these," she says.

Throop smiles, the kind of smile grown-ups make when they think you're being cute but ridiculous. "What kind of fool do you take me for? You first. Hand me the charts; I let your sister go."

Frankie looks at me, nervous.

Just at that moment, toward the back of our boats, there's a loud splash, startling all of us. Robbie pops up out of the water, takes off his mask, and shouts. "Savvy, you did it! I can't believe it but it's right here! We've found the *Queen Anne's Revenge*!"

Throop looks at me and smiles, a thin, wry smile. "That's all I came for, Savannah. I'm not a monster. I have no plans to hurt a small child. I just want what's rightfully mine." He goes inside his cabin, looks at his own chart and his screen, and quickly pages through a book. All the while Jolene stands shivering and looking terrified on the side of his boat. He writes down something and then comes back out to her. He gives us a polite little bow.

And without a word, he helps Jolene step across to our boat. Kate has a towel waiting and wraps her up tight. He doesn't mention the charts again.

Then Dunmore Throop pulls up his anchor and leaves.

"Who the heck was that guy?" Robbie asks as he rocks in the wake of Throop's boat.

I'm frozen, staring at the back of Throop's boat as it gets smaller and smaller in the distance, my fingers gripped so tightly around the railing my knuckles hurt. "This cannot be happening."

"He tricked us," Frankie says as she helps dry Jolene, giving her hugs and kisses.

Peter sits on a bench. "He won."

I shake my head. I refuse to believe that. "No one won yet."

"But Sav, he's going to come back. With help."

"Throop is going to get our treasure?" Jolene asks, her voice wavering through chattering teeth.

I turn and put my hands on Jolene's wet shoulders. "No, Jolene. This isn't over yet." I turn and yell toward the sunset. "You won't get away with this, Throop!" I turn to Frankie. "We have to do something!"

She throws her hands up in the air. "Right now I'm drying off our sister. You know, the one who fell into the ocean because of you?"

Kate tries to stand between us. "Let's try not to get—"

"*That* was an accident!" I yell. "I'm sorry, Jolene! You know it was an accident, right?"

Frankie moves her away from me. "An accident that could have ended up way worse."

I throw my head back and groan. Frankie is missing

the point entirely. "She's fine. She just got wet." But even as I say it, her terrified little face sticks in my mind. I go over to her and crouch down. "I'm sorry, Jo. Forgive me?"

She gives me a little nod but backs herself into the cabin to sit down.

Peter and Kate give Robbie a hand getting back on the boat. As he takes his air tank off, he says, "Hey, y'all, stay calm. Don't worry about that old man. We've got all the proof we need right here." He hands Kate a small film camera he had hanging around his neck.

I don't think Robbie understands how serious Throop is about getting the *Queen Anne*, but I don't argue because he hands Peter a black and rusted round object about the size of a softball, which is what really gets my attention.

"You had an underwater camera with you?" Kate asks.

"Of course," Robbie says as he removes his flippers. "I got great shots. I'll bring the film in to be developed and we should have proof in a week!"

"But you didn't even totally believe us," I say.

"No, but I didn't totally not believe you either."

Peter turns the round object over in his hands. "What is this thing?"

"It's a cannonball, dummy."

"I knew it!" I shout and rush over to Peter to get a better look.

"They're buried all over the seafloor. Shipwreck stuff

everywhere, dude. I had to grab something!" Robbie says.

Everyone rushes Peter, scrambling for a turn to hold it. Frankie first, Jolene tries but needs some help, and then even Kate turns the ball over in her hands. "This is the most amazing day ever," she says.

I wait until last and sit down on the bench with the heavy ball in my lap. Blackbeard himself might have held this very cannonball.

"You can keep it, Savvy," Robbie says.

"Really?"

"If it wasn't for you, we wouldn't be out here at all. So as far as I'm concerned, it should be yours. I'm sure everyone agrees."

Everyone nods.

"Grandpa would have loved this so very much."

Frankie sits next to me. "It would have been his greatest accomplishment."

"If only we could tie ropes to the ship and drag it home, too," Kate says.

"Speaking of home," Robbie says. "We have missed our opportunity to get there before dark."

"We should get moving, then," Frankie says.

"But we can't just leave the *Queen Anne*!" I say. "We have to claim it somehow."

Frankie sits on the other side of me. "We may not get the whole ship, but we're keeping that."

"Why are you talking like that?" Robbie says. "No one else is getting this thing, are you kidding me?"

"How can we stop Throop?" I ask. "He's got the exact coordinates now. All he has to do is get his crew in here. They have everything they need to bring it to the surface."

"Yeah?" Robbie says. "Well, all we need is a radio. Peter, the call signals for the Coast Guard are on the board in there. Call them and say 'May Day.' "

Peter goes in and calls them.

"That'll get them here quicker than you can say crap on a cracker," Robbie says.

Jolene bursts out in giggles. "That's gross."

Robbie grabs a blanket from one of the storage benches, wraps it around Jolene, and rubs her shoulders. "Here, make sure you stay warm. They're probably going to ask how you fell in. We probably shouldn't mention y'all were playing pirate battle up here while I was doing all the work down below."

Just as Jolene sits back down on the bench, a loud *chop chop chop chop* sound in the distance suddenly gets louder and closer. Fast. And before we know it, a giant red-and-white helicopter is nearly on top of us, so loud and so powerful I have to cover my ears with my hands. The SS *Dare* rocks and water sprays out in all directions.

Everyone ducks and holds on for their lives.

Lost at Sea

The blades of the chopper are so powerful I feel like my ears are going to get sucked out of my head. Quickly, a small towing boat with several Coast Guard on board pulls up alongside us. The helicopter lifts and finally leaves, and then a loud voice comes over a speaker. "Prepare to be boarded."

Frankie, Jolene, and I squeeze together a little bit. My mouth is so dry I'm not sure I'm going to be able to speak.

Two men in blue uniforms come aboard our boat. Their names—Dunn and Burns—are on the front of their shirts and they both have guns and handcuffs. "The Dare family?" Dunn asks. We all silently nod.

"Are we going to jail?" Jolene whispers. I elbow her.

Turns out our family discovered we were gone—like gone from Ocracoke—before noon and called the Coast

Guard before we did. When Peter called in the May Day, they were already less than a mile away. Once we get our hearing back, and they assure us we're not going to jail, we all talk at once trying to explain what we found.

And they do not believe us at all.

"Look, dude," Robbie pleads.

"Did you just 'dude' me?" Dunn says.

"Sir, sorry," Robbie says. "Just wait until you see the pictures; we have proof!" He looks at me like he wants me to show them the cannonball, but I keep it hidden under a cushion. I don't know if we can trust these guys.

They laugh at us. "A shipwreck. That's a new one. Usually when kids are partying out here, they can't come up with anything that creative."

"We already told you," Frankie says. "We were not partying."

"Sure you weren't." They both laugh again. "Even if you did find a shipwreck, do you know how many are out here?"

"Nearly three thousand," I say.

"Exactly," Burns says. "So what makes you think you found the one Blackbeard the pirate sailed?"

"Because we're pirates too!" Jolene yells. I'm not sure that's the best thing for her to say, but since they just laugh more, I figure it doesn't matter; these guys simply don't believe us.

Kate leans over to me. "Are you going to show them the cannonball?"

"I'm afraid they won't give it back. Besides, Robbie was wrong. They clearly can't help us anyway. It's not them we have to prove this to, it's our parents."

Dunn hitches up his pants. "Look, kids, whether you found a pirate ship or a bathtub, there's nothing we can do about it. Besides, your parents are all waiting onshore and worried. We need to tow you in."

"Let's go." Burns waves his hand to show us the way to their boat. "Technically we could confiscate this stolen vessel, so if you ask me, you're getting off easy."

"Thank you, sir," Robbie says. We all get off the SS *Dare* and onto the officers' boat to be driven to our doom. I think about all the possible ways I can try to convince our parents of what we really found, but I'm not fully prepared when we reach the harbor and all our family, and Kate's mom, are lined up across the mainland dock. None of them looks particularly happy to see us, although I can see a lot of relief in Mom's face as she wrings the railing with her white-knuckled hands. Uncle Randy looks as if he might laser me with his eyes. I've never felt like I had so many enemies in my life.

"Oh man, we are in for it," Robbie says to Peter. "I'm not taking all the blame here."

"I'm not going to let you," Peter says. "This was our idea. You just helped."

"We're all to blame," Frankie says.

Kate takes my hand. "Yeah, we're in this together." Then she takes Peter's.

"Pirate oath," I say.

Once we get off the boat, the officers talk to our families, and then we each get pulled aside by our own parents and everything happens so fast I can't get a word in anywhere. There's never been so many parental lectures in one place at one time in the history of the world. Kate's mom seems mostly relieved but not very happy about me. At all. She guides Kate away and to the car before I can say goodbye.

I overhear Uncle Randy say something about how he's going to have to come back another time to haul the boat home and make Robbie pay for it. He also takes the camera. "This better still be working!"

When Robbie tries to explain what's on it, Uncle Randy won't even let him talk and he starts ushering the family to the car. He roughly throws the camera into the trunk. "Uncle Randy, wait!" I say. "Throop was there too. He knows now. He's going to get to the *Queen Anne* first!"

My uncle whips around and gives me a look worse than the angry-big-sister look of death. "Then Throop gets it."

Aunt Della buckles Will into his car seat. "Randy, enough. Let's go home."

I watch as their car pulls away. Peter half waves and frowns out the back window. I hardly hear anything else as my parents say the same things they always say about how we're supposed to tell them where we are, and yes, just as we thought, we're grounded for life.

"But Dad!" I say as he leads us to the van. "Isn't finding a pirate ship grounds for exclusion?"

"You know what, you're right," he says sarcastically. "Finding a pirate ship would be. But leaving the house before dawn, lying to your parents, stealing your uncle's boat, and driving it four hours down the coast is not."

"But I have proof!" I say. "On the boat. I was trying to tell you before Uncle Randy—"

"You're not getting back on any boat any time soon. Life, Savvy. Don't make me say it again or I'll double it."

"You don't understand!"

"Not another word."

I get in the van and scrunch down in the farthest back seat on one side, Frankie on the other. Jolene falls asleep in about thirty seconds and everyone is silent.

"He doesn't believe us, does he?" I whisper to Frankie.

Frankie doesn't say anything, just rests her chin in her hand and stares out the window. I think that's a no. Eventually Frankie falls asleep too. A little while into the ride, I think Mom and Dad think I'm also asleep, because I can hear bits of their hushed conversation.

"She seems convinced they found it, Jack. We need to hear them out."

"Even if it is the right wreck, what are we supposed to do about it?"

"Just believe them."

I take this as my cue to interrupt. I unbuckle and make my way to the middle seat, where I sit beside Jolene. She doesn't even stir. I put the seat belt on and lean forward. "If it *is* the right wreck—"

"Oh! Savvy," Mom says. "You startled me. Are you buckled?"

"Yes, Mom, I'm buckled. If it is the right wreck, and I know it is, all we have to do is get a crew there before Throop. The charts were a little off, but we wrote down the exact coordinates before they towed us in."

Dad shakes his head. "It doesn't work like that, Sav. It should, don't get me wrong. If you and your cousins found it, it seems like you should get to claim it. But it's much more complicated than that. We don't even *have* a crew like Throop does. And you don't get to truly claim an artifact like that. Even if Throop gets it, it would go to a museum."

"He's sneaky. He'll get to search it for treasure before anyone even knows," I say.

"I suppose that's possible."

I sit back, arms crossed. "None of this even makes any sense. Grandpa set us on a *treasure* hunt. Why would he lead us to something we can't have?"

Dad glances at me in the rearview mirror. He looks sad. "I don't know, tiger shark. Do you understand why I wasn't so sure about this from the beginning? Your grandpa was just—"

"Maybe just a little lacking in judgment," Mom finishes for him.

"That's putting it lightly," Dad says.

I rest my head on the back of the seat. "This isn't over yet, Throop." But tears leak out of my eyes anyway because I'm really afraid that it is.

"Savvy?" Mom asks.

"What?"

"You mentioned earlier there was proof on the boat. What did you mean by that?"

"A cannonball. Robbie dove down to see the wreck. It wasn't very deep. And he came back up with a real cannonball."

Mom looks at Dad with a serious expression. "Jack?"

"No." Dad shakes his head. "Don't even say it."

"How can you say no? They've been working on this for weeks. They deserve something to show for it."

"What are you saying, Mom? You think we should go back and get it?" I sit forward and bounce on the seat a little bit. "Can we?"

"We've been driving for two hours, Anne. Jolene needs to change into dry clothes. You want me just to turn around?"

"Dad, please! I know exactly where it is. I hid it under the cushion. I can be fast!"

"Come on, Jack. Don't tell me you're not curious? We can stay overnight at a motel."

"This is bonkers," Dad says. But then he slows

down the van, spins it around, and heads back to Cape Lookout.

"Yes!" I punch the air.

Jolene startles and sits straight up. "Did we win?"

"Not yet," I say. "But we're going to."

Back to the Beginning

As soon as we get back to Cape Lookout, I burst out of the van and run down the dock. It's dark but the harbor is lit up plenty for me to find the SS *Dare,* jump on board, and retrieve the cannonball from behind the bench cushion. I run back to my family to show them.

Dad weighs it in his hands. "Wow. Heavier than it looks, isn't it?" He passes it to Mom and says, "All right, well, we have your proof. I'm no expert but I'd say that shot is pretty old. Let's get ourselves set up at the motel and in the morning we'll contact the local maritime museum and see what they say." He messes my hair and smiles.

"Thanks, Dad."

"No promises. But you're welcome."

By the time we all settle in the room and share a pizza, and Jolene gets showered and wrapped in blankets and passes out on Mom and Dad's bed, it's close to midnight. Frankie and I crawl into bed and I fall asleep thinking how excited the museum will be to see what we found.

The next morning seems to arrive in a blink. Sun streams through the window and I can smell my parents' coffee. Frankie is already in the shower and Jolene nibbles on a banana.

"Good morning, sleepyhead," Mom says to me, and tosses me a banana. "You slept late for you!"

I yawn and stretch. "I guess I was really tired."

"Yesterday was a long day for all of you, I'm sure."

"Especially me," Jolene says. "I almost drownded."

Mom hugs her. "Yes, I know that was scary."

I put my banana on the table and climb into Mom's bed with Jolene. I give her a huge hug. "I'm sorry, Jo. You know it was an accident, right? I'd never do anything to hurt you on purpose."

"Fortunately, you all had the sense to wear life jackets," Dad says.

"Robbie made us," I say.

"Well, good for Robbie. That gives me hope." Dad sips his coffee, and Frankie comes out of the bathroom. "Savvy, do you want to jump in next?"

"Can we just go straight to the museum? I don't think I can stand waiting."

"Well, I don't think we can stand smelling you in the van," Frankie says, smirking.

Mom interrupts before I can say anything rude back. "It doesn't open for another hour anyway, Sav."

"Fine."

Once I'm showered and everyone has a bite to eat, we finally head to the museum. The cannonball rests in my lap the entire way and my stomach is in knots. *Will they let me keep it? Is it worth anything? Is it really Blackbeard's? Could I go to jail for stealing it?*

Turns out, they can't tell us anything officially. Except that I'm not going to jail. Whew!

"This is a wonderful find," Mr. Campbell, the museum curator, says. He's a small, balding man with a kind smile and soft voice. "But you'd have to leave it with us for some time to analyze it in order to confirm the year."

Dad looks at me. "What do you think, Savvy?"

"How long?" I ask.

"Maybe a couple of weeks," he says. "We have special people who do that kind of work and they rotate through different museums. No more than a month at most."

A month sounds like forever to me. But if it's the only way to prove the shipwreck is the *Queen Anne's Revenge,* then it's what we have to do. I hand the cannonball to Mr. Campbell.

"We'll do our best," he says. "And it will be in very good hands." He smiles and then takes down some information from my parents while my sisters and I look around the museum. There are artifacts from all kinds of shipwrecks. Bowls, utensils, weapons, shoes, and even scraps of very worn paper with fancy handwriting. Plus, cannons and cannonballs everywhere because they last the longest underwater. It reminds me of Grandpa's collection at home, how he took such good care of all the artifacts he found, whether they were worth something or not. The *Queen Anne* would have been his greatest discovery. Nothing would have made him happier. It makes sense to me now that it might have been only the ship he wanted us to find and nothing to do with gold or jewels or any kind of pirate treasure.

Still, I can't help but wonder if there is treasure on that ship or somewhere else on Ocracoke. Part of me is still really hoping there is.

Frankie, Jolene, and I are looking at a giant painting of a pirate battle on the ocean when our parents come find us. "We're so proud of you girls," Dad says. "Despite the very bad judgment in taking Uncle Randy's boat, we're proud to have such smart, determined daughters."

My sisters and I smile at one another. I look up at Dad. "Thanks, matey."

When we get home, late that afternoon, the first thing I do is call Kate and Peter and tell them everything that happened. Peter says his dad has calmed down but it might be a while till he can hang out. And Kate says her mom is still a little upset. I know I'm going to have to apologize to them and I will, but first I have to check something out.

The entire drive home, all I could think about was Grandpa's original poem to us, the one he gave to Mrs. Taylor at the historical society months ago to hold for us.

North, South, East, and West
Around the island awaits a quest.
Hidden tools and clues are found,
Pirate treasure throughout your town.
Riddles and puzzles you've always known;
Stories I've told you as you've grown.

Start with the map and trust your youth,
Sometimes the obvious is the truth.
And remember what I've said of thee:
Strength together, a cord of three.
When in doubt, please remember:
I'm with you always and forever.

"North, South, East, and West," I say out loud. And something clicks. I go over to the map and look at the three spots I have circled and then get my sisters.

"What is it, Savvy? Why are you still studying this?" Frankie asks.

I smack my hand on the map. "The park: west. Our house: east. The cemetery: south."

"Okay?"

"There's nothing for north."

"I'm trying to put this all together," Frankie says.

"Don't you see? We thought a clue was missing and it is. Grandpa said in his poem there were treasures all over the island. And so far we found something at each of those spots—a key, the box of documents, and the name of our ancestor, who is also an ancestor of Blackbeard's."

"So there should be something somewhere north waiting for us too? It sounds like a stretch," Frankie says. "But maybe."

Jolene peers at the map. "But what could it be?" Her finger traces the compass arrow to the north, which is Silver Lake Harbor.

I write the words as I talk. "The answers to the three riddles: elbow, window, short. They weren't only hiding places."

Frankie sees it first. " 'E,' 'W,' 'S'! Like east, west, south!"

"Yes!" I grab her arm and shake it because I'm so excited. "Each letter stands for a location *and* a compass direction! So there should be a riddle with an answer that starts with 'N' that leads us north and gives away the specific location."

"Savvy, easy on my arm . . ." Frankie's eyes search the map. "Did Grandpa even have a riddle that had an answer with the letter 'N'?"

"I only remember three," Jolene says.

I nod. "I thought there were only three, at least three he

told us the most. There must be another one he assumed we'd remember. Or he has it coded somewhere."

We stare at one another for a while, like it might jog our brains. Frankie chews on the inside of her cheek. I get up and pace a bit. Jolene flops onto the couch. But none of us can recall a fourth riddle.

"I know I'm right about this," I say. "We have to think harder."

"We will," Frankie says. "You're the hardest thinker I know."

The Brothers Gain All

One night about a week later, we're sitting in the living room together while Mom and Dad watch some boring news show. Frankie's working on homework, Jolene puts together a puzzle, and I'm curled up in a chair with one of Grandpa's journals, searching, as always, for a clue to the riddle. Reading about his adventures makes me long for a life just like his, an adventure I was already on until we were rudely taken over by the scallywag pirate Dunmore Throop.

We still haven't figured out the fourth riddle even after asking Peter. It's very frustrating, but I'm also not as worried this time because I'm pretty sure Throop thinks the hunt is over.

"If I wanted to be a real treasure hunter," I ask the room, "would I have to go to college?"

Dad looks at me over the top of his glasses. "It would

probably help. History and archaeology would both come in handy."

"Did Grandpa go to college?"

"No, he didn't. Grandpa went to the navy and then came home and started a family. But he was an independent learner. I mean, look at these shelves. The man never stopped reading."

"I could be like that," I say.

Dad smiles. "You already are, but—"

Mom shushes us. "Jack, look." She points to the TV.

The bottom of the screen says "Cape Lookout Shipwreck Discovery, Oceanic Recovery Crew Association." The reporter, dressed in a green windbreaker with a little yellow anchor on the chest, braces herself in the wind and sea spray as she talks. "Pamela Parker here with ORCA's president, Dunmore Throop, the man and company responsible for discovering an ancient shipwreck believed to be the *Queen Anne's Revenge*, belonging to the famous pirate Blackbeard."

I jump out of my seat. "What?! He didn't wait one second, did he?!"

"Savvy," Frankie hisses. "Shhh!"

The reporter continues. "Tell me, Mr. Throop, what all was involved in this discovery? How big was your team?"

The camera focuses on Throop's skinny face and green cap. "Well, Pamela, it wasn't easy. Many years of research and dive expeditions. We have twelve on the

ORCA team, but on discovery day it turned out to be just me, believe it or not."

"Wow, that is impressive. What made you set out on that day, to that spot?"

"Honestly, a hunch. Sometimes you have to follow your gut. I'd known the general area of the grounded ship for a long time, and I thought after the hurricane came through last month it was a good time to get back out and search. Storms can unearth shipwrecks, seeing as they change the ocean floor, and it seems my hunch was lucky." He sneers at the camera as if he's looking right at us. Laughing at the entire Dare family.

Even though I knew this was going to happen, I can't contain my rage. "He can't get away with this!" I stomp around the room. "We told the Coast Guard what we found. We have the cannonball for proof. We have to at least tell them who *really* found it! He doesn't get to claim it!"

"Savannah," Mom says, "I know it's disappointing, but there's nothing you could have done about this. Professionals would have had to come in and verify it either way. He might have the only crew in the area to even do it, so you'd have to rely on him anyway."

"I don't care!" I point to the TV. "That is Grandpa's ship. That is our family's ship! Right, Dad? If we're descendants? It belongs to us!"

"Savvy, I don't think it works like that. And as of

right now we have no real way to prove that a bunch of kids found it first."

"We talked about this happening, Sav," Mom says.

"I didn't think it would be so soon! And I didn't think it would make me this mad. But I'm mad. I want Grandpa to have the credit. He had the location first; he just couldn't get there on his own."

Frankie clears her throat. "Well, Mom, Dad, don't we have all the proof we need?"

"What do you mean?" Dad asks.

"We can't prove that *we* found it until we get the results on the cannonball, but we can prove Grandpa had the location before Throop. We have all the clues and documents."

"Yes!" I want to kiss Frankie, but she'd probably hit me. "Of course! We can show them all the stuff we have."

"At least it would stop Throop from getting credit he doesn't deserve," Frankie says.

"And buy us some time for the museum to get back to us!" I say, nearly jumping up and down.

Mom and Dad agree to put together a package to send to the museum, since that's the only contact we have.

But after we send it, weeks go by with no word from the museum.

In school, my sisters, Peter, Kate, and I discuss what the fourth riddle might be and what Throop might be up to. Peter has no idea what happened to the underwater camera, and Uncle Randy refuses to talk about that day. When I pass Robbie in the hall, he sometimes gives me a small smile. Other times he ignores me as he always used to.

Slowly, the treasure hunt fades from our conversations. At night, I stare at the ceiling and wish I could hear Grandpa's voice once more telling me the final clue.

The days get colder and the island quieter. We can't do ghost stories anymore because there aren't enough visitors in the campground. We hoped to do something at the Fall Festival later this month, but I lost my motivation. Most days are a little too cold and windy for skateboarding, so Kate and I spend more time in the attic when we hang out, but the Star Board has been retired, pushed under the couch indefinitely. I rolled up the Ocracoke map and placed it in a tube in the closet. Dad fixed the floorboard. Now we play Uno and Clue. Sometimes Frankie and Jolene join us. Although Frankie spends most of her time with Ryan.

I start to think that our whole adventure will simply be a family secret that will probably fade away or become a legend. I'm mostly okay with that, because Grandpa also had to deal with no one believing him for a very long time, the fact that sometimes treasures aren't found. On Kate's suggestion, I start my own journal to document everything that we did in the last few months.

Throop dropped the case against us and our house,

probably because he got the ship. It wouldn't matter now anyway since we have the deed, but at least my parents don't have to go to court to prove it.

But just when I think it's all over for good, we get a phone call. Mom answers and when she's done, she tells us everything. Her face is so excited I can hardly sit still on the kitchen stool as she explains. It was a woman from ORCA, the same company Throop works for. Her name is Beth Armstrong and she told Mom they are getting ready to raise parts of the shipwreck and take it to a museum on land. And she'd like all of us to be there, if we want.

"How did she know about us?" I ask.

"I don't have any idea."

"Maybe from the Coast Guard who were there that day," Frankie says.

"What happened to Throop?" Dad asks.

Mom shrugs. "Don't know. She didn't mention him at all."

"We're going to go, right?" I ask.

"How could we not!" Dad says. "I feel like we owe you that much at least, Savvy."

Turns out Peter's family is also invited and surprisingly are also going. Kate's mom won't let her go, so I promise to take a lot of pictures for her.

When we arrive at the harbor, a ton of very smiley people are waiting for us. "Welcome!" One cheery woman steps toward us and reaches out. "Beth Armstrong." She shakes all our hands. "It's so nice to finally meet you all, to finally meet the Dare family."

"Likewise," my mom says. Everyone looks a little confused as to why Beth Armstrong is so happy to meet us. But we follow along, letting her and her team lead us to a huge boat that's going to take us out to the shipwreck site where they've been preparing to lift the *Queen Anne's Revenge*, or at least some cannons and a section of the ship.

At the site, there are several other boats and a really big crane built right into the ocean with cables and ropes everywhere. Beth says, "Our team has been diving and retrieving artifacts from the ship for weeks and they've fortified the largest section of the hull that we believe is sturdy enough to bring to shore.

"It's a tricky thing, the timing here. The *Queen Anne* has been preserved underwater for hundreds of years. She could simply crumble, or maybe we will be able to salvage the largest section, but surely once she's exposed to oxygen and the longer she remains exposed, the more damage she takes on." Beth looks at all of us, and her eyes land on me last. "But we've done it before and we will do everything we can to take care of her."

"What will happen after you lift it?" I ask. "Where are you taking it?"

"We have a museum where we can continue to preserve it and hopefully rebuild more of it so it can be on display for everyone to see," she says. "In fact, I think you met one of the staff people there, Mr. Campbell?"

"Wow," Jolene says. "That must be a big museum to fit a whole pirate ship in it!"

Beth smiles. "It's a good-sized one. Now before we start, there is one more thing we have to talk about." She glances at Uncle Randy, who nods. Then she brings over a box that had been sitting on the bench nearby and hands it to me.

"What's this?"

Uncle Randy pats my shoulder. "Open it, Savvy."

I set the box on the floor in front of me, open the flaps, and gasp. Inside is the wooden ship Grandpa had been carving when I was younger that disappeared years ago. I pull it out and my mom whispers, "How in the world? I haven't seen that since you were eight years old!"

The ship is finished and beautiful. *Queen Anne's Revenge* has been carved into the side in loopy, intricate letters. On the side a little metal plaque has been added to the back of the boat that reads:

NOVEMBER 27, 1996
RESURRECTION OF THE *QAR* DISCOVERED
BY CORNELIUS FRANKLIN DARE AND
HIS GRANDCHILDREN: FRANCES, SAVANNAH,
JOLENE, ROBERT, PETER, AND WILL.

Aunt Della leans over my shoulder. "We just added Will so he wouldn't feel left out. Hope that's okay."

Frankie and Jolene take turns examining the boat and exclaiming how beautiful it is. I can hardly talk. "I . . . I don't understand. Where did you find this?" I look at Ms. Armstrong. "And how did you know it was really us who found the wreck?"

Ms. Armstrong clasps her hands. "I'm so happy you're happy. We secured this beautiful piece from Dunmore Throop before he was fired and then Mr. Campbell contacted us about a certain cannonball and several sensitive documents. But I believe your uncle can tell you the details." She smiles so big it looks like it hurts her cheeks. "I'll give you a few minutes and then we'll get this ship moving."

I turn to Uncle Randy, who has tears in his eyes. I don't have to say anything; he tells us the entire story.

"Robbie's photos," he says. "That was the only proof I needed. We came down here, what was it, honey, two weeks ago? Met with Beth, gave her the photos, and she showed us the wooden ship. Basically we told her the entire story of how you girls have been hunting for the last two months for something that I, foolishly, didn't think existed. We didn't want to say anything to you and get your hopes up if nothing would come of it."

He walks over to me, bends down, and looks in my eyes. "I am sorry, Savannah, for the way I treated you."

"Thank you," I say. And he gives me a big hug.

Aunt Della wraps her arm around Uncle Randy when he stands back up. "They had been suspicious of Throop for a long time. He'd been involved with a few shady discoveries he tried to claim as his own, so it didn't take much to persuade them to kick him to the curb. And Beth said the carved ship was in his office and he'd once bragged about tricking an old man out of it, trading it for a useless antique ring."

I hug the wooden ship close to my body. Funny that Grandpa knew the ring *was* useful. But why would Throop want the ship so badly? It was just one of Grandpa's many carving projects, like the walking stick Peter got. "Where do you think Throop is now?"

"Beth told us he has family in Florida, so maybe he went there. Or maybe he went back up to Boston." Uncle Randy shrugs and puts a hand on my dad's shoulder. "Maybe he'll get focused on treasure hunting somewhere else and leave poor old Ocracoke alone."

"Randy, I don't even know what to say." My dad looks near tears as he hugs his brother. They thank each other, and Uncle Randy says, "Let's not worry about Throop. I think he's done."

Ms. Armstrong heads back our way and asks, "Are you ready to watch a pirate ship fly?"

I place the wooden ship back in the box, close it, and tuck it in the cabin for safekeeping. Then we all crowd the side of the boat. And wait.

After what seems like hours, they finally start lifting, a very slow and gradual rolling of cables and ropes. The crane groans with weight and I wonder just how big the section of the ship will be, until suddenly the frame of a kind of metal box begins lifting up. The water rolls off to the sides as though making way for the huge contraption meant to carry the *Queen Anne's Revenge* to safety.

Inside the framework, we can just make out the shape of a real wooden ship, and although there are gaping holes and muddy, splintered wood covered in barnacles and centuries of mud and sand and seaweed, it is a beautiful sight. I glance over to Dad and Uncle Randy, who have their arms around each other. Dad covers his mouth as he watches the massive artifact lift from the water. Uncle Randy teases him for being sentimental. But they both have tears in their eyes. Water continues to pour off the sides and out from underneath as the entire section rises into the air. The mast and sails are long gone, leaving only a hulking, broken body behind.

But in my imagination, I can see the entire flagship, white sails billowing, Blackbeard's famous black-and-red flag flying, next to a Jolly Roger crossbones. The pirate himself stands at the helm, sword in hand, beard black as night, and vows to never be taken down. I know that he did countless horrible things as a pirate, but in some weird way he will always remind me of Grandpa. Always on a journey. Never giving up.

Always believing there was something out there for him to find.

"Me too, Mr. Teach," I say. "Me too."

One Last Riddle

April 1997

Spring break brings a lot of vacationers back to Ocracoke, so to prepare for the onslaught of cars and extra people, the ferry runs extra hours, the stores open back up longer, the campground is alive again, and we all embrace sharing our village with the world. Mostly by showing people all there is to love on our island, but also figuring out how to make money off everyone.

Kate and I have written at least six more scripts for ghost stories, and Mom has even allowed us to move our business to the house, now officially on the historical registry as the residence of Blackbeard's descendants. We've been asked a hundred times to open up as a real museum, and Mom and Dad are considering moving all our personal belongings to the top floor and doing just that on the first floor—displaying all of Grandpa's artifacts, books, journals, and maps, and a very special cannonball from the *Queen Anne's Revenge* for tourists to see for themselves what a real treasure hunter does.

But we haven't gotten that far yet because Mom isn't so excited about the idea of strangers in her house all the time. For now, she's okay with our telling ghost stories on the porch and allowing visiting kids to see some of the treasures, as long as they have permission.

Jolene makes a huge banner out of a roll of paper that reads:

WELCOME TO GRANDPA CORNELIUS'S
FAMOUSEST MUSEUM OF PIRATE TREASURE

Frankie helped her with the spelling, but no one had the heart to tell her "famousest" is not a word.

I sit in my room and try polishing a new ghost story while I wait for Kate and Peter to show up, but my focus is elsewhere. Ever since the day we watched ORCA pull parts of the *QAR* out of the ocean, I've thought about how one thing doesn't add up. Grandpa thought he'd deceive Throop, throw him off track by giving me and my sisters all his research. But Throop was onto him, and he wanted to get Grandpa's wooden boat. Clearly Throop thought the boat was a clue to the hunt. Or maybe had a clue in it. Probably the very clue we've been missing.

I pick up the boat. It's about as heavy as the cannonball. Turning it over in my hands, I check in every nook and cranny of the carving for some kind of special sliding chamber or door. But it seems completely solid. I get a magnifying glass out of my desk and continue to look until suddenly I see a teeny mark carved into the stern, just peeking out from behind the little nameplate Beth Armstrong put on. It's so hidden it looks like part of the design, but I have to check it out.

I hate to take off the nameplate, but I can always put it back. Using Grandpa's old knife, I pry it up. And underneath there is a letter.

N

And more letters. Very tiny and so easy to miss. But there are four in all. N A M E.

Which is funny because that's where the ship's name would traditionally be.

"Name?" I say out loud to the empty room. "Whose name?" I say it a few times and suddenly the riddle hits me. I remember it all at once.

It belongs to you but other people use it more than you do.

Your name.

"My name?" No, it can't be me. It has to be something bigger. Grandpa's name? I have no idea, but just like Jolene pointed out months ago, the only significant thing that's north is Silver Lake Harbor. I race out of my room and down the hall to Frankie's room, where she and Jolene are finishing up the banner.

"You have to come with me right this minute!"

Jolene salutes me.

But Frankie shakes her head and colors in the letters on the banner. "Savannah, we're going to the Fall Festival. Besides, aren't you—"

"You have to trust me. The clue was on the wooden boat that Throop stole. I think he assumed the name was 'Hort,' which is why he was at the cemetery that day, but I think he was wrong."

Frankie and Jolene both give me strange looks. "What name? What are you talking about?"

I explain what I found on the boat, and the riddle I remember. "I don't know exactly what we're looking for but I think it's at the harbor. I think we'll know it when we see it. Please, just come with me to check it out."

"There are no names at the harbor. This doesn't make sense," Frankie grumbles, but she gets up from the floor and helps Jolene up too. We get our skateboards and head over to Silver Lake. There are a lot of people around for the festival, so we attempt to act normal. Jolene tries to whistle. I poke her shoulder.

"What?" she asks. "I'm acting like I'm minding my own business."

We scour the harbor, but the only names we see are the names on the boats. Grandpa couldn't have hidden anything on someone else's boat—that doesn't make sense. After several minutes, we sit on a bench overlooking the choppy water.

"Maybe it's someplace else north," Frankie says. "I mean, the ship wasn't on Ocracoke."

I put my head in my hands and groan. "That would stink. I want it—whatever it is—to be here."

"Well, me too, but do you see any names anywhere around here?"

I shake my head.

Jolene points. "I do!"

I look up and see the big landmark sign at the far end of the harbor. We run over and read it:

EDWARD TEACH

NOTORIOUS PIRATE CALLED "BLACKBEARD."

LIVED IN BATH WHILE CHARLES EDEN WAS GOVERNOR.

KILLED AT OCRACOKE.

1718

"That's a lot of names," Frankie says. "How do we—Savannah!" she yells at me as I sit on the edge of the dock right below the landmark sign and start to slide into the water. "What are you doing?"

I don't answer, I just follow my gut as I plunge into the cold water below us, gasping when I surface. "Just. Hang. On." I take a deep breath and dive under the dock itself. Then I surface again, below where my sisters are standing, and spit out salty water and a bit of seaweed. The things we do for adventure.

I can see Jolene peering through the cracks. "I'm okay!" I tell her. I can't explain to them how I know what I'm doing; I just know. It's how Grandpa explained all his adventures. He followed something inside himself. He'd had all the research, the maps, the clues, but the rest was up to his own curiosity. Now I'm curious. In fact, beyond curious. And there is no other name that Grandpa was more obsessed with than Blackbeard.

It's hard to stay afloat under the dock with the waves crashing in. More than once they slam me into the poles. But I keep searching all the corners and ledges of the underside of the dock. Above me Frankie whimpers a bit. "Oh, Savvy, this is a bad, bad idea. Please come out!"

"I'm okay!"

"You should be doing this at low tide!"

"Just don't let anyone see me!"

I feel like I've looked in every possible corner until suddenly I spot it, tucked up under the decking on top of the piling. There's just enough room to squeeze in a box. It's tied very tightly, but I have Grandpa's knife in my pocket. Holding on to the piling with one hand and slicing at the rope with the other, I finally free it, duck under the water with it, and come up sputtering.

Frankie helps drag me out of the water. "It's a good thing you're so strong," I say when she gets me on my feet.

"It's a good thing you're so scrawny!" she says, trying to catch her breath. "What did you find?"

I lead them away from the harbor, and even though I'm dripping wet and it's chilly out, my adrenaline is pumping. We duck behind a large bush and I show them the box.

"It's a tiny treasure chest!" Jolene squeals and covers her mouth. "With a lock!"

"And I bet you know how we're going to unlock it." I barely even get all the words out before we make a mad dash for home. When we get back, Peter and Kate are just arriving.

"Perfect timing!" I shout. "Come on!"

Kate tries to ask why I'm all wet, but we just run into the house in a rush. All of us tear up to the attic and I faintly hear my mom ask us to slow down, but I don't listen.

The key is packed away in a box with all the other stuff Grandpa left us. I dig it out, we all gather around the box, and I stick the key into the lock. "Are you ready?"

Everyone nods. Jolene rubs her hands together.

I turn the key, and the lid unlatches. Inside is a plastic bag with a small velvety pouch inside. It's dry. I open the pouch and pour out dozens of silver coins.

Everyone gasps. "Are they real?" Peter asks.

I pick one up. It has numbers, symbols, and Spanish on it. "I think these are pieces of eight, the kind of Spanish coins that pirates would steal." I grab a handful. They're almost soft and buttery in my hand, musically clinking together. "You know what this means, right?"

Jolene squeals, "We're rich!"

"Well, maybe, but where do you think these came from?" I look at Frankie.

She reaches inside the pouch. "Wait, Savvy, look." She pulls out a piece of folded paper. "It's from Grandpa!"

"Is it another code?" Jolene asks.

Frankie shakes her head. "Not this time." And she reads to us.

To my darling granddaughters, the Dare sisters,

If you're reading this, you've gotten further than you know. But there is still a long way to go. Decades ago, our ancestor Benjamin S. Hort raided the Queen Anne's Revenge where it lay at the bottom of the ocean and stole the captain's treasure right from his cabin walls where it was hidden! I documented this, copying his pages in one of my journals, which you've likely found by now, and I know there is much more where this comes from. However, if you decide to abandon the hunt, I would not fault you. Following a treasure hunt your grandfather builds versus one a true pirate-treasure hunter like Hort builds are two very different things. There could be untold dangers ahead. You may want to claim this bounty and call it a day. And then again, maybe not. I love you all greatly. Always be true to yourselves. And never stop searching.

Love, Grandpa

"In his cabin walls," Frankie repeats. "That's what the ghost was trying to tell us."

"And there's more where this came from," I say as I rub my thumb over a coin. "This isn't over yet. We have to find that journal." Everyone nods. I look at my sisters. At Kate and Peter. "And you know what else this means, don't you?"

"What?" Kate leans forward on her knees.

I go over to the trunk of pirate clothes and pull out costumes for everyone and a plastic sword. "It's time to officially swear you in to the pirate oath." They change into the ruffled shirts and poofy pants, bandannas and tricorn hats. We look like a true band of pirates.

I face Kate, place the sword on her shoulder, and raise my hand. "Do you, Kate 'The Skate Pirate' Roberts, solemnly swear to be a true and rightful guardian of the Dare family treasure and whatever else awaits us?"

She raises her hand. "Oh, I totally do!"

"You have to repeat it all," Jolene whispers.

"No, it's okay this time," I say. I turn to my cousin. "And you, the Honorable and Fair Peter Dare. Do you solemnly swear?"

Peter raises his hand. "You had me at the key. I'm in this for life."

Everyone puts their hands in the circle. I stand with the sword in the air as I speak. "Dare family, descendants of Edward Teach and loyal guardians of the treasure, and friends of the Dare family: We will never let anyone break us apart and we will search as long as it takes us, even for the rest of our lives, to the ends of the earth—"

"Savvy? We have a fall festival to get to," Frankie says.

"And lunch," Jolene whispers.

"Shhh!" I say. "Don't interrupt greatness."

Frankie hangs her head back. I'm sure she rolls her eyes.

I finish our oath. "To the ends of the earth, for the rest of our lives, if that's what it takes, to find the remaining treasure of Blackbeard the Pirate." Everyone raises their hands in the air and we all shout, "Yo *ho*!"

Frankie and Jolene scramble out to get ready for the festival. Peter and Kate leave together smiling and teasing each other about who can skate the fastest. And just before I switch off the attic light and shut the door, I turn back and take a look around the crow's nest, and I whisper a thank-you in my heart to the one and only Cornelius Franklin Dare, keeper of codes and secrets, master of riddles and maps, woodworker and storyteller. But to me, a loving grandpa, my best friend, and true pirate.

Author's Note

The *Queen Anne's Revenge,* Blackbeard's famous flagship, sunk off the North Carolina coast near Beaufort Inlet in 1718, only months before Blackbeard was killed at Ocracoke. In 1996, an archeological dive group called Intersal, Inc. discovered the shipwreck, and they have been slowly recovering parts of it ever since. Saving a shipwreck is a very long, arduous process, and although in this story the Dare sisters get to see a big section of the hull lifted out of the water, the real process of bringing artifacts to the surface takes place over many years. As of today, they have recovered hundreds of thousands of artifacts from the shipwreck site. The Queen Anne's Revenge Conservation Lab in Greenville, North Carolina, displays many of these findings, including cannons and cannonballs, anchors, pewter dishes, bottles, trade beads, and much, much more. You can visit the museum or go on their website, qaronline.org, to see photos and learn more history about this ship and Blackbeard.

One other really cool fact is that it's believed Blackbeard removed any truly valuable treasure from the *Queen Anne* before she sank. And nothing was found on the *Adventure,* which was the ship he had when he died. Some believe the treasure is still out there. And maybe someday *you* can become a treasure hunter and go find it! As long as Savannah Dare doesn't beat you to it.

Acknowledgments

Cheers!

Once more to my agent and friend, Linda Epstein, who continues to light the way with nothing but professionalism and commitment not only to a career, but to sharing stories that empower, encourage, and entertain. Here's to more adventure!

And again to Captain John Morgan (and your genius puzzle brain), who gallantly handed the wheel to Captain Melissa Warten in an excellent transfer of power. No finer editors could be had. Melissa, thank you for welcoming me with warmth and encouragement. You made the change in direction seamless, and I can't wait to see what we accomplish together.

To the entire team at Imprint who saw this book through near to the end, and to my new team at FSG who I'm thrilled to be finishing up with. I especially look forward to future collaboration on projects full of adventure and heart. May we sail the seas together for a long time!

To Christine Almeda, who illustrated both covers of *The Dare Sisters*, thank you for your beautiful renderings! I'm always amazed by the art process, and you brought these girls to life in a new, fun way for me.

To Peter Vankevich and the *Ocracoke Observer*, for

your dedication to the village and your support of *The Dare Sisters*. I've been reading your paper for a long time, and it's always been a wonderful way to feel connected to the place I love.

To Ashley and Dave Burns, who gave me valuable insight to Coast Guard rescues—you guys rock!

To the residents and businesses that make Ocracoke a destination unlike any other: Thank you for putting up with tourists like myself and for sharing your home with so many.

To all my sweet readers who have been on this treasure hunt with Savvy and her sisters: Thank you for telling me what you love and hope for with this story. What a privilege it has been to hear from each and every one of you who has reached out!

To my friends and family who continue the voyage with me, who stay by my side even when I reach land, only to set sail again.

And, as always, to Joe, my partner in all things piratical and otherwise. Thank you for continued days of laughter and love, brainstorming and plotting, and for making sure that every time I say "I quit," I don't.